KATZENJAMMER

GREENWILLOW BOOKS

An Imprint of HarperCollins*Publishers*

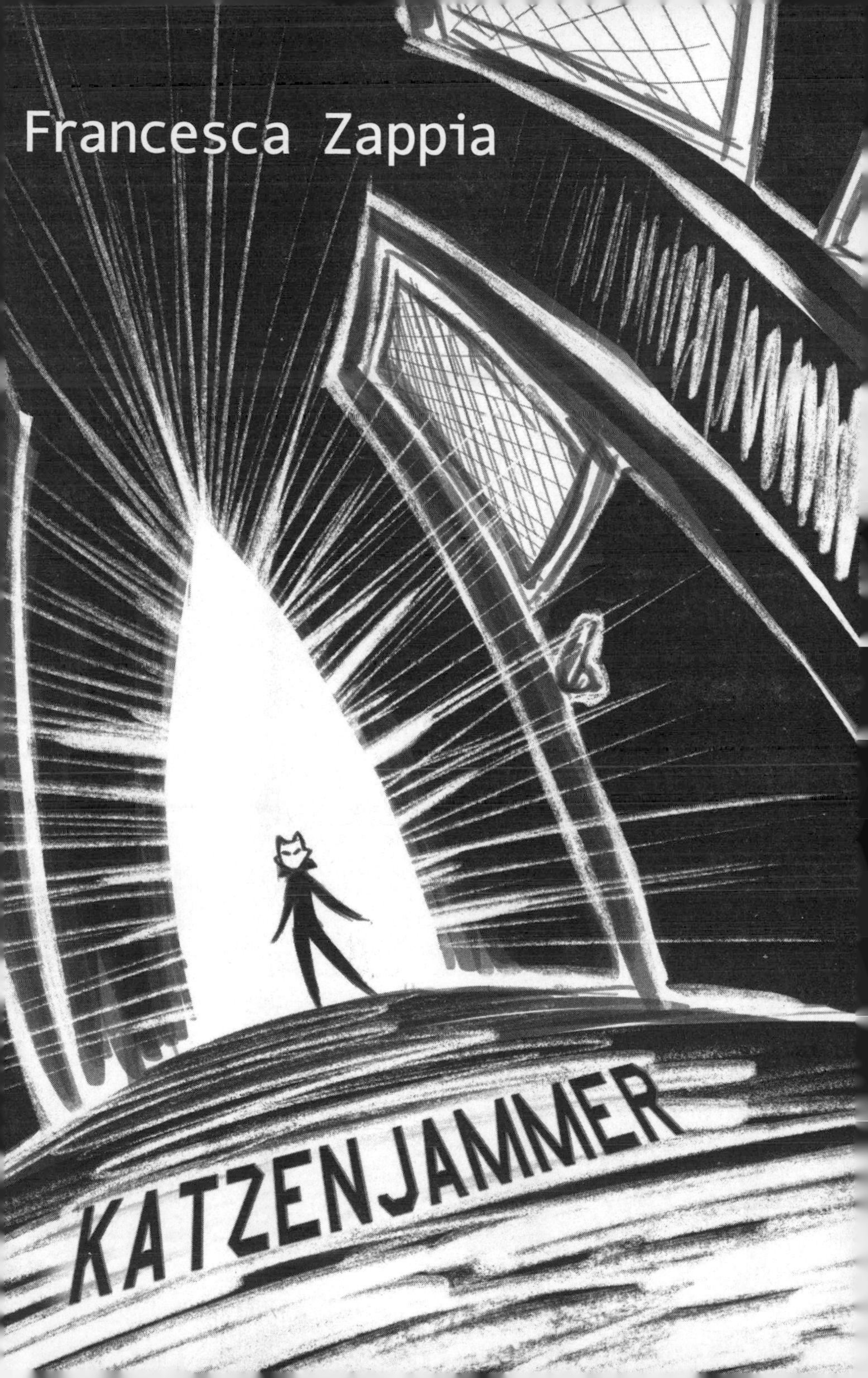
Francesca Zappia
KATZENJAMMER

Katzenjammer
Text and illustrations copyright © 2022 by Francesca Zappia

The text of this book is set in Charlotte Sans Book and Charlotte Book.
Book design by Sylvie Le Floc'h

Library of Congress Cataloging-in-Publication Data

Names: Zappia, Francesca, author, illustrator.
Title: Katzenjammer / written and illustrated by Francesca Zappia.
Description: First edition. I New York, NY : Greenwillow Books, an imprint of HarperCollins Publishers, [2022] I Audience: Ages 14 up. I Audience: Grades 10–12. I Summary: In chapters that alternate between the past and the present, Cat slowly recalls her life before she and her classmates were trapped inside School, where half of them are mutating, everyone is fearful, and self-destruction seems to be the only means of escape.
Identifiers: LCCN 2021055294 (print) I LCCN 2021055295 (ebook) I ISBN 9780063161658 (hardcover) I ISBN 9780063161665 (ebook)
Subjects: CYAC: Bullying—Fiction. I Memory—Fiction. I School buildings—Fiction. I School shootings—Fiction. I High schools—Fiction. I Schools—Fiction. I Horror stories. I LCGFT: Novels. I Horror fiction.
Classification: LCC PZ7.1.Z36 Kat 2022 (print) I LCC PZ7.1.Z36 (ebook) I DDC [Fic]—dc23
LC record available at https://lccn.loc.gov/2021055294
LC ebook record available at https://lccn.loc.gov/2021055295
22 23 24 25 26 PC/LSCH 10 9 8 7 6 5 4 3 2 1
First Edition

Greenwillow Books

For everyone who changed,
and everyone who never had a chance

I cannot make you understand.
I cannot make anyone understand
what is happening inside me.
I cannot even explain it to myself.
—Franz Kafka, *The Metamorphosis*

EYEHOLES

My eyes are gone.

That figures.

I stare into the mirror in the girls' locker room for a full two minutes, examining the new emptiness in the eyeholes of my mask. Then I wait another minute before I jam a finger two knuckles deep into my eye socket.

Nothing there. I should be scrambling my own brains.

Question of the day: What's stranger—trying to scramble your own brains, or wishing you could?

Whatever. It's not like I need eyes anyway.

I dunk my head under the sink faucet and let the water run over my hair. I once used the showers to clean up, but now they only spray blood. Not just when you turn them on, but all the time, hot and thick and sticky, and it weirdly reminds me of that opening scene in *Carrie*. Red rain hits the tiles and I imagine a chorus of girls chanting *Plug it up, plug it up*.

I wish the showers would plug it up. It reeks.

I stare at myself in the mirror and wonder how I got here, stuck inside School, with the plumbing full of blood and my face looking like this.

I don't remember.

None of us do.

The moment I think *I don't remember,* the first memory comes unbidden and crystal clear.

I was six. I sat in the middle of the school gymnasium while they sorted us into our classes and passed us off to our teachers on the first day of first grade. A Wonderful Day of Firsts. The first time I wore the blue corduroy dress with the overall straps. The first time I was around a lot of other kids my age without Mom or Dad there.

My name was called. I knew my name then, but not now, and in the memory it's a garbled noise. A finger pointed to my destination, a group of kids in the far corner. Mr. Lahm's class. I clambered to my feet—adorable in my shiny saddle shoes—and hurried to join them.

Six girls, five boys. I sat down beside a girl with curly brown hair and purple pants. She said hello and told me her name was Priscilla, but I could call her Sissy, because Priscilla sounded like the name of one of those fancy white cats that eat food off glass plates. I thought about telling her that Sissy wasn't very good, either, but I wanted to make friends.

The boy sitting on Sissy's other side kept looking at me, so I thought he might want to make friends, too. But when he saw me staring back at him, he put his fingers in front of his eyes and waggled them in opposite directions, like his eyes looked different ways. Him and the boy next to him started laughing, and it didn't sound very friendly.

Every time he looked at me that day, he did that with his fingers.

That was the clearest part of the memory. How horrible he looked, making fun of me.

CAT

Well. I guess I do remember something.

I lather up my hair with the hand soap from the dispensers, rinse it out again, and dry it off with the locker room towels that have thankfully remained blood-free. Then I wipe the water droplets off my mask. The edges of the towel dip into my empty eye sockets once or twice and I jump every time, even though I don't feel anything.

The others may be concerned that I've lost my eyes. I need to remember to be careful when I see them, so they know I'm still me.

When I'm clean—when my head is clean, since I've had issues taking my clothes off lately—I neatly fold the towel on the shelf above the sinks, comb my blackglove fingers through my blacksheet hair, and recheck my mask one last time to make sure nothing else has changed today.

Nope. Still a cat.

Of all the ways students have changed inside this school, a cat mask made of hardened flesh is on the boring end of the spectrum. I can't make the expressions I used to, and now I guess I don't have eyes, but at least I am still myself.

I can't say as much for some of the others.

.2.......

The second memory comes all at once, instantly.

Ryan Lancaster was the name of the boy who made fun of my lazy eye on the first day of school. The other kids stopped laughing after a while, so he moved on to other things to get their attention.

One of his targets was Sissy. Everything about her. The size of her perm. The size of her stomach. The amount of hair on her arms. How she liked her peanut butter sandwiches cut right down the middle instead of diagonally.

One day in gym class, we had to play kickball. Sissy moved to the plate as the teacher rolled her the ball, and when she kicked it, it soared over the infield, past the outfield, and hit the fence. Our team cheered; Sissy ran to first base as fast as she could, which wasn't very fast at all.

Not fair! Ryan Lancaster yelled from the outfield, instead of running to get the ball. Sissy moved on to second base.

Why is it not fair, Ryan? the gym teacher yelled back.

Because, only *boys* can hit the ball that far, but she's on the *girls'* team! She's not a girl, she's a boy!

Sissy stumbled halfway between second and third. I'm not a boy! she yelled back.

Liar!

I'm not a liar!

Sissy's a boy! Ryan called.

No, I'm not!

The chanting started. *Sissy's a boy! Sissy's a boy!*

Quiet, all of you! the gym teacher yelled. The field fell silent. I sunk against the chain-link of the backstop and wished I could disappear. The teacher rounded us up and herded us back inside. I trailed at the end of the line with Sissy behind me, her face red and tears dribbling down her cheeks, though she bit her bottom lip in a valiant effort not to cry.

I thought I might be able to say something to make her feel better, but all I could think was *I'm so glad it's not me.*

INHALE

When I leave the locker room, the long hallway behind the gyms is a little wider than it was before, the ceiling a little higher. The doors have spread farther out along the wall. School is inhaling. The entire building has stretched itself up and out like a tall man climbing from a tiny car. It's much better than when School exhales, because then we spend months crawling around constricted passageways and shrunken classrooms, the desks and chairs and file cabinets and bookshelves crowding in, and we hope we don't get stuck somewhere we can't escape.

Another plus is that when the hallways get bigger, they get darker. Makes lots of nooks and crannies to hide in. When the hallways are small, they're all superbright, and there's no way to avoid anyone. School is weird like that. I think it likes to mess with us.

What am I saying? Of course it likes to mess with us.

It trapped us here.

.3......

Why are the memories coming now?

I liked to draw. In fourth grade we had to take a different mandatory recreation class every day: Tuesday was music, Wednesday was gym, Thursday was library, and Monday and Friday were art. Art class was basically a paper and crayons party, but the teacher sat me in a corner of the room with a pencil and I drew the first thing that came to me—an owl perched on a tree made of hands.

Then Ryan Lancaster ran by, scribbled black crayon across my page, and said, It wasn't that good anyway, what are you angry about? The teacher made him go to the principal's office, but Ryan didn't seem upset about it.

School taught me that I liked to draw, but home was

where I could do it without protecting the picture at the same time.

Mom and Dad loved that I did art things. Well, Mom loved it, and Dad was okay with it, though he clung to the idea of me playing tennis. He wanted more championship trophies to add to his collection, but with my name on them instead of his. He never got them, and only complained about it on my birthdays and Christmas, when he and Mom presented me with another crop of sketchbooks, pencils, markers, brushes, paints, canvas. Everything I needed to empty my head of the images that grew there like parasites. Surreal landscapes, twisting hallways, subtle gleams in the darkness like knife edges at night.

They're all so dark, Dad said one day, watching over my shoulder as I worked at the kitchen table. Why don't you paint things like a blue sky, or a field of flowers, or a bird flying on a breeze? Something happy that your mom can put on the fridge.

She can put these on the fridge, I said.

Maybe just one flower? he asked.

There are no flowers where I live, I said.

CHAIR

It figures that the memories that come back to me now are the useless ones, the ones that explain nothing about how I got here, how we all got here.

I hug the walls and creep to the English hallway. I move carefully. I can't call out for Jeffrey because I can't risk alerting whatever might be out here. That's what School does. There is no speaking in the hallways out of fear of what or who will hear. Because there's always the possibility that the person who responds to you is not the one who wants to help.

My long-sleeved shirt and pants and shoes and gloves are all black, so I blend in well. Some of the others aren't so lucky—they changed in ways that are too distracting to ignore. But not me. Whenever I want, I disappear into the shadows. Even my eyes can't give me away now.

Mrs. Remley is the only one in her classroom when I arrive. Strange. Usually Jeffrey arrives before me. Like the rest of the building, the room is illuminated by vague sources of light just out of your field of vision; when you turn to look, the light changes. Mrs. Remley sits behind her desk, her varnish gleaming dully. I brush dust off her and scoot her up to the desk once again. Someone must have come in here and pulled her out without realizing who she was. But who, though? Jeffrey and I are the only ones who use this room. And Mrs. Remley rarely moves herself.

Footsteps sound in the hallway outside.

.4.......

I met Jeffrey in middle school.

It was a Tuesday.

The cafeteria was serving pizza sticks, and the cafeteria only served pizza sticks on Tuesdays. I was in line for pizza sticks behind a kid wearing a sweater vest. I was trying to comprehend the sweater vest when a group of boys in football shirts came up, said hi to Sweater Vest, and cut him in line.

They're going to eat all the pizza sticks! was the first brilliant thing out of my mouth.

Sweater Vest turned around. I'd seen him a few times in the halls but never paid attention to him. He had these big brown eyes and thick blond-brown eyebrows like honey caterpillars. Honeypillars. Like they could wrap you up and keep you warm on a cold winter day. They pushed together in the middle when he looked at me.

He said, I'm really sorry; you can go ahead of me.

Are you sure? I asked.

I was surprised because usually when a large group of popular kids cut in line, everyone pretended like nothing had happened and that was that.

He nodded, so I took his spot, and I got the last pizza sticks.

Later, I watched him sit at the far end of the same table with the football guys, off by himself. With nachos.

I tapped him on the shoulder and said, Do you want to sit with me and my friend? You can have half my pizza sticks.

He looked to where I pointed, to the table where Sissy sat with her back to the wall, picking the ham out of a chef's salad.

Sure, he said.

I said, My name's ( ), and I like pizza sticks.

He said, My name's Jeffrey, and I've never gotten any pizza sticks.

SQUARE

"**C**at! Oh, Cat, good, you're here!"

Jeffrey appears in the doorway to Mrs. Remley's room. I want to hiss at him to learn to walk more quietly. He turns the corner too tightly and his head grazes the doorframe, making him recoil. He's gotten pretty good at avoiding corners, but every once in a while he'll get excited and forget that his head is a cardboard box. He holds a hand flat against its short side and blinks at me, dazed.

I feel a jolt in my chest whenever I see Jeffrey, a warmth that reassures me we will be okay even though we are stuck in this place. The jolt is entirely about who Jeffrey is and not at all about what he looks like now. Jeffrey's face is a crude crayon drawing, just two big circle eyes and a rectangle mouth filled with square white teeth. When he blinks, his eyes flip between open circle and closed line, like an animation with only two frames.

He straightens his blue sweater vest and looks around like someone might have seen his blunder, though he knows Mrs. Remley would never make fun of her students.

"Cat," he begins again, a little slower. "It's terrible—you have to come see—"

He stops when I take a step toward him, and I know I've put myself in enough light for him to see my eyes. Lack of. Straight eyebrow lines appear on his forehead, furrowing a cardboard ridge between them. The sides of his rectangle mouth curve downward.

"Cat?"

"I'm okay," I say. My voice is too loud inside these dusty classroom walls. "What do I have to see?"

His shoulders slump and he flattens a hand over his face, over one closed eye. "God, Cat. I thought you were gone."

"Nope," I say. "Still here."

He peeks over his hand. One of his pupils is colored in; the other is an empty circle. "You can see?"

"I can see whatever it is you need to show me." Now I'm less concerned about my eyes and more about Jeffrey rushing in here. Jeffrey doesn't rush. He might get anxious, but he does it with the genial air of a game show host trying to shine a shit prize. Jeffrey is the calmest sea, because he has to be, because he's the one who keeps the peace between us.

All of us—the ones who have changed *and* the ones who haven't.

Most of us had been together since middle school.

By "been together," I don't mean we had been friends since middle school. I mean middle school was the first time we were all in a building together. And by "us," I mean all of us, not just me and Jeffrey and Sissy and Ryan Lancaster, but the others, too. I remember that much.

I remember sitting down to watch the announcements and seeing tall, pale Julie Wisnowski reading off the school news in first period. I remember no one in class listening, because Lane Castillo was too busy recounting her various weekend adventures in an obnoxiously loud voice. I remember a river of faces passing in the hallway, familiar but distant, people I saw every day and would never know.

I remember the small caravan of almost-friends I traveled with from class to class, and I remember them mostly because I think we all knew we stuck together out of necessity. One of us alone in the hallway was a target. All of us together were just more faces in the river, moving slowly but steadily toward the sea, where we'd be free.

I didn't mind not being good friends with any of them. Sissy and I were the kind of friends who didn't really see each other outside of school, but while we were there, we had each other's backs. We'd known each other too long not to do that much, at least. But she was best friends with Julie, so I was on my own most of the time. Until Jeffrey came along, I mean, because post-Jeffrey life was much better than pre-Jeffrey life. And Jeffrey was one of those people who was in all of your classes, but you never noticed him until you looked. The quiet kid who sat in the middle of the room and kept his head down and did all his work and wore a sweater vest.

A lot of us were like that. And by "us" I mean *us*. Not *them*. A lot of people think what happens happens because we ask for it—because we're too loud, or too strange, or too persistent. But most of us are like Jeffrey. Trying to keep our heads down, trying to get out alive, but they find us. The Lane Castillos of the world. The Raph Johnsons. The Jake Blumenthals. They found us in the river, and they chose us for their long, sick games.

FRAGILE

I follow Jeffrey to the courtyard. I am quieter than him. I hear distant sounds in the hallways before he does. I won't let either of us be caught unaware.

The four hallways that enclose the courtyard expand and contract with School's breathing, but the courtyard itself always remains the same size and shape. There is a tree in one corner with a wooden picnic table underneath it, and weeds choking the rest of the small square space. The sky overhead has been replaced with a blinding whiteness that sneers at us when we dare look up.

The Blinding spills through the many windows that line the hallways around the courtyard. When my eyes (ghosteyes? noeyes?) adjust, I see the crowd gathered in the middle of the courtyard, backs to the windows. El, Pete, West, more, more of us than I've seen together since we arrived here. We stick to our own lairs for the most part. Twenty, maybe thirty kids. The number seems to change each time I look.

Jeffrey holds the door open for me. Heads turn. Silence falls.

Silence except for the sobs that echo through the courtyard.

I step toward them. They part for me like fallen leaves, looking at my eyes, where my eyes should be. In the middle of their circle I find Sissy curled over a prostrate body. She whips around and looks up at me, her tentacle curling in shock.

"Cat," Sissy sniffles. Her tentacle, for once, goes still. She leans back, and I see the body beneath her.

Julie Wisnowski, class president.

Her porcelain head has been cracked open on the stone path. Long locks of blond hair swim in a pool of blood. Two blue eyes stare up at me, but one is still attached to her face and the other is in pieces, sinking into the red. Her body—the parts of it that are still intact—is limp. Her feet have broken off at the ankles and one arm rests at the base of the west wall, like someone threw it there.

Julie was fragile, but she was not a klutz. At least not enough of a klutz to break her own arm off and leave it twenty feet away from where she smashed her head open. She loved this courtyard, loved looking up at the blinding white sky and thinking how sad it was that none of us had mutated wings.

Something found her here. Something tore her apart, and it must have hated her.

"Cat?" Sissy says again, this time with fear in her voice. My eyes are gone, so she does not know if I am me. Looking down at Julie's broken body, I am not sure if I am me, either.

"Who did this?" I ask, and my voice is as cold as my blood.

.6. . . . .

Memories spark.

Flares of light in the darkness.

I am remembering on purpose. I am remembering for a purpose.

Julie Wisnowski was one of those students who cried when she got a bad grade on a test. Algebra, biology, English. It didn't matter what class. She didn't get bad grades often, but when she did everyone knew it. Once she cried so hard in history, Mr. Lommel gave her enough extra credit to bump her up a letter grade. Sometimes I was convinced it was an act. Sometimes I was convinced I'd like her more if it was an act. At least then it would be purposeful, some kind of survival tactic rather than a breakdown of will and an inability to accept failure.

Julie was one of us. She was a face in the river, but maybe more visible than most because she was our perennial class president.

We were in upper-level algebra together in seventh grade, with some of the eighth graders. Julie was better at math than me, but that didn't mean much—neither of us were very good, and Julie's tests, no matter how hard she studied, usually came back with a nice big B minus. I was fine with my Cs, but Julie's Bs always had her down for the count for the rest of the day.

When we got midterms back, before Julie had even checked her grade, Raph Johnson orchestrated it so that the entire class turned around and watched her. Julie didn't notice until she'd already flipped her paper over, and then it was too late—the waterworks had begun. She looked up to find the class watching her, smiling because they'd gotten exactly what they wanted, and then she looked to me, beside her, as if I could stop them, or give her a better grade, or help her stop crying.

But I could never help anything. Why would I want to? Helping meant making yourself a target.

I was good at hiding back then, too.

FROSTBLOOD

I am not the most imposing of us, or the fastest, or the strongest. But right now I might be the angriest. I am beginning to remember, and even though I don't know everything yet, I do know that it is not fair that we should be attacked like this. I didn't like Julie that much, but this shouldn't have happened to her. She isn't the first of us to die, but she should be the last.

The others look at me as if I might be able to do something. I don't know why; I have never been their leader, have never pretended to be. I stare back at them and wonder if they can tell that I see them. If they know I am remembering us as we were before.

We are the changed ones and one of us has been murdered. We won't be safe until we find out who is responsible.

Sadness dilutes my anger as I gaze down at Julie's body. I believe that this was done out of hatred, but I don't know how so much hatred formed. I clench my hands at my sides so I don't try to rip my mask off, and I repeat, as slowly and calmly as I can, "Who did this?"

"No one knows," Sissy says, voice wobbling.

The others stay silent. Sissy's tentacle slithers up her sleeve to hide. Someone's joints hiss, the sound of shifting hydraulics. Lamplight eyes blink, so bright they obscure the face of the person they belong to. One boy's skin chitters like a squirrel until he hugs himself. None of us knows anything. We don't know why we're here. We don't know why we changed.

I look to Jeffrey.

"We heard her scream, and the noise she made when she hit the ground," he says quietly, glancing down at Julie. "Sissy, West, and I got here first. The courtyard was empty."

"It could be . . . " West begins, then stops himself. When he speaks again, his voice is choked. "It could be Laserbeams."

"It could be any of the lost students," says El. "Or someone from administration."

"It could be *anything*," I snap, and they all shut up.

. 7 . . . . .

I never realized my friends were my friends until it was too late.

Like Sissy. I made it to third grade before I realized we were friends. It wasn't as if either of us had ignored or hurt the other; I was just oblivious. Or didn't think about it. Most of the time she was "the one who doesn't make fun of my eye/clothes/packed lunch." Then she invited me to her birthday party, and I was the only one who showed up, and I finally got it.

This didn't happen with Jeffrey. I remember that day in middle school, sitting down at the lunch table with my pizza sticks, introducing Jeffrey to Sissy, splitting my pizza sticks and giving half to him. He smiled and gave me half his nachos. As he reached over to drizzle cheese on them, a bolt of lightning came from the sky and fried my brain, and when the smoke cleared, the words *Jeffrey Blumenthal's Best Friend* were permanently scorched into my forehead. And I loved it.

I don't know why it was important, though.

Why is it so important that I remember this?

BOUNDARIES

I pull Jeffrey out of earshot.

"Do you think it was Jake and the others?" I ask.

"Maybe," he replies. "But they don't come to the east wing. This is our place, and administration is theirs."

"I don't trust them not to break their own boundary lines," I say.

His little worried eyebrow lines appear again. So depressingly far from the honeypillars they used to be. The memory of the honeypillars is so clear to me now, even with all of the other images flooding back into my head. "There's no evidence that anyone from administration did it," he says.

"Then who did? Mark?" I say it with as much sarcasm as I can muster.

"Mark doesn't move when you're looking at him and runs away as soon as you look somewhere else," says Jeffrey, as straightforward as always. "He can't talk, but we don't know for sure that he's dangerous—"

"He's a wanderer," I interrupt. "He's lost. You know there have been others like him, and until they died or disappeared, they attacked anything that moved. Are you going to start telling me Laserbeams isn't dangerous, too?"

Jeffrey shuts up.

I go on. "Whether or not Jake and the others did this, we have to check in with them. There are only so many options, and if they didn't do it, then that means they're not safe, either. We need to tell them. They can help us figure it out; they can help us search."

Jeffrey's face goes unnervingly still while he deliberates.

Then he says, "Fine. I'll go talk to them."

"*We'll* go talk to them," I say.

Jeffrey knows better than to argue.

I turn back to the others. They are still watching me, waiting, as if I have answers they don't.

"Don't walk the hallways without a friend," I say.

.8. . . . .

We grow older.

Years pass.

The memories hit me like punches.

There were people in the river who helped guide the currents.

Julie was one of them. I don't know if she liked doing it or not, or if she even realized what she did, but she was class president, and even if you didn't know her personally, you knew who she was. Depending on how you looked at it, she was either a guidepost or a scapegoat—are you the butt of jokes? Do you often find yourself lacking confidence and humiliated? Just look at Julie, who becomes the butt of everyone's jokes when there's a test to take, yet still pulls herself together and does the announcements every day.

Jeffrey was one of those people, too, but in a different kind of way. He was the kind of kid no one bothered because he was self-assured and good-natured so he didn't have any weak spots. The first time I heard someone make fun of his sweater vest—lightning-forehead-best-friend day, coincidentally—was the first time I ever saw someone shut down by a smile. Some kid caught him on the way out of the cafeteria and asked how long Jeffrey's mother had been dressing him. Jeffrey smiled at him, friendly as hell, and the boy stood there in stunned silence as Jeffrey walked away with me to my locker.

Jeffrey could talk to anyone. Nerds, jocks, theater kids, punks, it didn't matter. He was a universal translator. Currents flowed around him all day long, absorbing that positive energy. I wished I could be like that. I wished I didn't have to be such a parasite leeching off him, because that was what I felt like most days, in the beginning. When he wanted to be my partner in class, it felt like he was doing it because he knew I didn't have anyone else to partner with. When he said he liked my drawings, I only heard white noise.

Then one day during the summer between seventh and eighth grade, the landline rang and my dad picked it up and said, (   ), the phone is for you! It's a boy, says his name is Jeffrey.

I stood in the garage with a canvas and a paintbrush dripping black paint and the image of a winding fleshy tunnel like the inside of a throat. I stared at my dad on the other side of the door to the kitchen, holding out the phone with a bemused look on his face.

Jeffrey Blumenthal? I asked.

Jeffrey Blumenthal? Dad said into the receiver. He listened, then said to me, he says it is, but if you'd rather he call himself something else, that's fine, too.

My feet took me forward and I pushed my way through the screen door into the kitchen and grabbed the phone.

Hi? I said.

Hey, Cat!

Definitely Jeffrey. Jeffrey always called me Cat.

Sorry for the random call, he said. I would've texted you, but you don't have a phone. As you know. Are you busy today? My brother Jake is having a big cookout for his football conditioning friends at my house, and I was kind of hoping you might want to come over so I don't have to deal with them by myself.

He said it the way Jeffrey always said things: positive and to the point with a side serving of humility.

I started to ask him why he didn't invite ___ or ___ or ___, only I couldn't think of any names to fill those blanks. When I tried to think of who Jeffrey hung out with, I only came up with me. We had some mutual friends, but I'd never heard of Jeffrey spending time with them outside of school.

Are we doing anything today? I asked my dad, who had taken a seat at the kitchen table to continue reading the paper.

Your mom is working on her new bonsai exhibit all day, and for the foreseeable future I'm sitting right here reading this paper, Dad said. Why?

I held up the phone and said, Could you take me to Jeffrey's house?

CATHERINE

It feels as if a projectionist is inside my head, playing my life on a film reel, only showing me excerpts at a time. As Jeffrey and I walk through the halls toward administration, I try desperately to remember more. Maybe if I know how we got here, I can figure out how we can leave. If we can leave, no one else has to die.

The hallways groan. In the distance there is the sound of footsteps. They come nearer, then fade away.

I glance at Jeffrey, who is busy looking over his shoulder, checking the hallway for others. For the lost. They are here, somewhere, wanderers like Mark. We never know if the footsteps are theirs.

Jeffrey's left hand runs along the edge of his face, feeling the contours. Again. Preoccupied. I won't get a straight answer out

of him when he's like this, but it doesn't stop me from wanting to ask the same questions for the hundredth time. *Do you know how we got here? Do you have any ideas for getting out?*

Do you remember my name?

Maybe Cat is my real name. Maybe it's not.

But as long as I never have to hear Jake Blumenthal or his friends say *Here, kitty cat* ever again, I will die happy.

.9......

The night of the party.

Jeffrey lived in a brick ranch-style house with a big backyard, two dogs, his mom, Cindy, and his older brother, Jake. Cindy had big hair and big lips and big makeup, which was why she made a living selling all of those things. She liked having a lot of people in her house, you could tell.

Jeffrey's dad had left them. Jeffrey didn't like to talk about it.

You're Cat! Cindy hugged me before I got through the front door. Jeff said I'd know you when I saw you. I'm so glad you were able to come—he hates being alone at these cookouts. He should be in the backyard. Just go straight through here, past the kitchen.

She had dark hair and green eyes and looked nothing like Jeffrey; I had to stare at her face for a moment before I saw any resemblance. She directed me into the family room, where several parents lounged in chairs and on a couch, watching a football game on a low-sitting television while a fan in the corner blew air at them. I hurried past and into a kitchen stocked high with junk food. The sliding door to the back porch stood wide open. Outside, a flock of soon-to-be-freshman boys played a game of pickup football while more parents talked at folding tables scattered around the yard. A man stood at a grill beside the porch, flipping burgers with one hand and nursing a beer in the other. Citronella candles disguised as tiki torches lined the yard.

Cat!

Jeffrey sat in a lawn chair to the side of the porch, flanked by two old, slobbering Saint Bernards. For once, Jeffrey was wearing a T-shirt and shorts. It really shocked me that he had leg hair. It wasn't that I hadn't expected it, just that I'd never considered the idea that Jeffrey's legs weren't khaki pants.

I suddenly felt overdressed. Mom had offered to buy me a dress so I could look nice for once in my life, even though I would rather have been wearing shorts and a T-shirt, too. Dresses were fine, but not when I was at a party with a group of high school boys, and not when I was the only girl.

Jeffrey jumped up.

Sorry, he said. I would have come to the door, but I didn't know when you'd get here. Do you—do you want anything to drink? Right now all we have is soda. And water, but it's tap water, so if that's okay . . .

Don't worry about it, I said. I'm fine.

Jeffrey smiled. I'm really glad you're here, he said.

Me, too, I said.

Then a football collided with the back of my head.

HERE, KITTY
CAT

Jake Blumenthal is the unofficial leader of the unchanged. When all this started—when we all arrived in School, one by one, with no memories of how we got here; when we began to change; when we realized our changes would eventually kill us and we could not escape this place—he took his band of merry assholes and built a fortress in the administration offices. They have a straight shot to the cafeteria for food, and they never have to go into School's spidering hallways, where we, the changed, live in fear of the wanderers.

Here's the story:

Jake and his band of jerks are scared of us.

End of story.

From what Jeffrey tells me—because Jeffrey's the only one

of us they *don't* find scary, the only one they will speak to for any length of time—they say we're changing because we've been "rejected," and if they come into contact with us, they'll start to change, too. And if they start to change, they'll never get out of School. Some of them think it's what happened to us that keeps us inside, as if School is a quarantine zone. They think they can escape by eradicating us, like an infection.

All of these theories are just fancy ways of saying they're terrified. I get it—I used to be scared of them. And maybe I still am a little bit. But just because my face is a cat mask doesn't mean I don't have as much chance of leaving this place as they do, with their soft skin and their mouths that open and their *eyes*. So whenever Jeffrey tells me one of Jake's theories, I file it away as bullshit and move on.

They're welcome to be scared of my footsteps in the dark.

.10......

The football. My head.

I remember being upright one second and on the ground the next.

The dogs barked and someone laughed and Jeffrey kneeled next to me, trying to help me up.

I'm fine, I said, holding the back of my head with one hand and blinking away the tears.

Sorry about that, someone said.

I turned to see Jake jogging over for the football. Tousle-haired, green-eyed, athletic, sun-ripened Jake Blumenthal. I'd seen him before, when he and his friends cut Jeffrey in the pizza stick line, when he walked past in the hallways, against the current. But now he was talking to me, directly to me, and somehow that made him more than an idea of a person.

I couldn't speak because I was sure it would be mostly puke that came out of my mouth, so I kept my lips clamped tightly shut and watched Jake take the football back to his friends.

Sorry. Jeffrey sighed. He didn't even apologize. He's a jerk.

It's okay, I said. It was an accident.

I didn't know if it was an accident or not, but I know I spent the rest of that night on the outskirts of the party with Jeffrey, watching Jake.

Why do I have to remember this? Why is this important?

ADMINS

The administration offices have been fortified with electric fencing and about a thousand wooden spikes crafted into a barricade. I'm always concerned about the spikes. Where did they come from? We used to spend seven hours a day molding our butts to metal and plastic. There wasn't enough wood around here to knock on.

The electric fence is less strange. School vomits out stuff like that all the time.

Jeffrey is kind of a pro at getting into administration. When we arrive, he rings the bell at the secretary's desk and tucks his hands into his pockets in his very best *Don't let me bother you, but I'm not going away* stance.

"Stop fidgeting," he says to me. "They'll never talk to us if you look so nervous."

"I'm not nervous," I say, wiping at my mask. I'm angry. I'm angry and I'm not leaving here until I know who did that to Julie.

The door slams open and Raph Johnson marches out, pointing a very large crossbow at our faces. Pointing at my mask, I should say, because no one in administration ever suspects Jeffrey of anything. Raph was a running back, compact and built for speed, and he still wears his football letter jacket except with the sleeves torn off like some kind of eighties action star.

"Identify yourselves," he says.

"It's us," Jeffrey says, because we're standing right there, and we spent years in school with Raph.

"I've got an itchy trigger finger, Jeffers," Raph says, "and your friend doesn't look so good."

"Fuck you, Raph," I say.

"Where'd your eyes go, *kitty cat*?" he asks.

"Fuck you, Raph," I say.

"Just want to make sure no one's been making any trips into Knifeworld."

"Why would we go to Knifeworld?" Jeffrey says.

Raph repositions the crossbow against his shoulder. "How are we supposed to know what you freaks get up to out there in the hallways? How do we know you haven't been hanging out with Laserbeams this whole time?"

"If you let us into your fortress, you wouldn't have to worry about that," I say.

He swats that comment away like a fly. "Why are you here?"

"We need to talk to Jake," Jeffrey says. "There's been an incident."

"To save you some time, I'll tell you what Jake will tell you." Raph lowers the crossbow enough to put on his best square-shouldered, flat-browed Jakeface. "Nothing that happens out there is any of our business."

I brush past Jeffrey, right up to the edge of the secretary's desk, close enough that Raph snaps the crossbow back into place in surprise. "Julie Wisnowski is dead," I say. "Someone smashed her head open and ripped her body apart. It wasn't any of us, so if you'd like to rule out any of the kids in administration, you'll let us talk to Jake."

By this point I'd already considered the fact that we might get into the administration offices but never come out again, because they will have killed us, too. But if Jake Blumenthal tries to kill me, at least that will give me an opportunity to get a few good shots at him first.

Raph must see the logic in my argument, because he finally lowers the crossbow and allows us around the desk.

.11.....

I thought that party was the longest night of my life.

After the football hit me, and Jeffrey accepted that I wasn't going to die from head trauma, we got food and retreated to the lawn chairs by the big slobbering dogs. There were only two chairs there, so I suspected Jeffrey had brought one over just for me. We drank too-sweet lemonade and swatted mosquitoes away from our legs, and I laughed when Jeffrey accidentally dripped mustard on his shirt. It was kind of nice sitting away from the adults and the football players, and I didn't even mind whenever someone walked up to Cindy and looked over at us and clearly asked who the girl was sitting with her son.

Probably too many times, Jeffrey had to pull my attention

away from the football game. I couldn't understand how they didn't get tired of playing, mentally or physically, but I was glad because it gave me more time to watch Jake without him noticing me watching him.

This had never happened before. I had never felt such a quicksand need to absorb a person, to be near him, to know everything about him. I saw him smile and imagined it was for me. Watching him move was hypnotic, even when he was only jogging back into position for the next play or shifting his weight from foot to foot. He made his friends laugh. He made the best plays. He was the one they all looked at when they needed a decision.

After a while the mosquitoes got too bad even with the citronella candles, so we all moved inside. Half the football players had to leave with their parents, so that left me and Jeffrey cooped in the corner of the living room with Jake and his remaining friends entranced by Madden on Jake's Xbox.

Jeffrey and I talked about movies we wanted to watch together and argued about the best theater candy. Sometimes Jake and his friends got too loud for us to hear over them, but neither of us suggested moving. Moving meant leaving the place where everyone was laughing and having fun, even if they were ignoring us. Moving meant missing out on the snack bowls and soda Cindy brought in for the boys, even though they were gone before we could get any. Excitement built up in my chest as Jake's friends left one by one, shortening the social hierarchy in the room.

We'd lapsed into silence and I had one big Saint Bernard head resting in my lap when Jake and his new best friend Raph dropped into the recliners beside us. Suddenly I had too much air in my throat. They ignored us for a while, or maybe didn't realize we were there, because when they did they looked surprised.

Hey, you're the cat girl, Raph said, making it sound like I was one step away from official Crazy Cat Lady status.

Jake kind of stared at me, like he wasn't really part of the conversation, and he didn't look happy. Raph had engaged us without Jake's permission.

What's your name? Raph asked.

I glanced at Jeffrey.

Cat, I said.

Raph laughed.

Don't you do those paintings they hang up in the display cases at school? Jake asked in an offhand way, trying to make it clear that he still didn't want anything to do with us.

I swallowed past the bubble of air in my throat.

Yes, I said.

The dark ones with all the dead stuff and the creepy landscapes? Raph asked. And the one where the teacher is turning into a bunch of bats?

Yes.

Why do you draw that stuff?

Because I like it.

But it's weird.

Everything is weird when you take it out of context.

Raph gave me a strange look; Jake's expression hadn't changed, but he somehow looked both more and less interested in the conversation than before. Jeffrey squirmed beside me. Jeffrey never squirmed. Jake glanced over at him with a look of disgust before turning his attention back to me.

Why do you keep staring? Jake asked.

W-what? I said.

Yeah, why are you staring at him? Raph said, too loud. He drew the attention of the few boys still playing Xbox.

I wasn't staring, I said.

Kitty cat was totally staring at you, Raph said to Jake.

Jake snorted.

Jeffrey tugged on the tiny sleeve of my dress and leaned close to me as he started to stand.

Let's go outside, he said.

Jeffrey had a talent for predicting when situations were about to go horribly wrong. I'd learned to listen to him.

TAXIDERMY

Administration is a colorful wonderland of safety and drug fumes. The long admin hallway is pumped full of music, with offices growing to either side like tumors. The offices are all open to reveal their insides, spaces full of pillows and silks, televisions that play only static, teenagers swaddled in smoke haze. A buffet of food from the cafeteria is set up in one room, because unlike a lot of us, they still need to eat. Another room has a gaming console hooked up, and two boys play a game where they are each cartoon characters with large cartoon weapons, trying to kill each other. The crowd around them cheers.

I vaguely remember a few of us playing this game in the Fountain Room, back when we had TVs there. Sometime between then and now the TVs disappeared, along with the games. We tried to live like they do here in administration, and we failed.

The secretary, Mrs. Gearing, is a printer that is constantly jammed. The school counselor, Mr. Sellers, a geometric design of a snake on the wall. Principal Mitchell grows in pieces from the hallway ceiling, stalactites dripping water from nowhere. Jake Blumenthal has made his nest in the principal's office. It is the only closed door, and it sits at the very end of the hallway, with three large words carved into it: *US OR THEM*.

Raph keeps himself turned partly toward us, crossbow at the ready, and knocks on the door. "Jake. Your brother is here."

Someone groans on the other side, and there's shuffling, and some cursing, and finally Jake yells, "Come in."

Raph shoves the door open. Jeffrey goes in first, then me. Jake's office is part bedroom, with a nest made of furs and pillows covered in furs, and a bear-pelt rug with the bear's head still on it. The bear snarls at us. On the other side of the room is a massive oak desk with feet shaped like dragon claws, torches on the walls, and more of Principal Mitchell hanging from the rocky ceiling. It feels a lot like walking into a caveman's den. An executive caveman. A caveman with a private yacht and a vacation home in the Bahamas.

Jake and his girlfriend, Shondra Huston, sit behind the desk, her on his lap, still disheveled from whatever. You'd think they'd have more decency, doing that stuff in front of the principal. Maybe they do it on purpose. When I glide out from behind

Jeffrey, Jake and Shondra leap to their feet, and Shondra procures a harpoon gun from beneath the desk. Before she can fire, Jake yanks the collar of her shirt, and the shot goes wide. The sound of the harpoon cracking the ceiling is oddly muffled—School doesn't like loud noises—but pieces of the principal rain down on me. Jake grabs the barrel of the gun before Shondra can reload and fire again.

"Get that fucker out of here!" she screams.

"What the hell are you doing?" Jake spits at Jeffrey.

"I may not have eyes," I say, "but I can still talk."

They ignore me. "Do you know what kind of poison you're bringing in here when you do shit like this?" Jake continues. Color rises in his cheeks. He looks so little like his old self without the easygoing smile that made most people love him, the light of amusement that once lit his face.

Jeffrey shrinks in on himself, his rectangle mouth with all his rectangle teeth turning down into a frown before his expression freezes. "You're putting us in danger, too. I let you come in here because you're my brother and because you've still got your senses, but it's things like this"—Jake jabs a hand at me—"that make me question if I can trust you anymore."

"Cat's still Cat." Jeffrey reaches out for my sleeve, tugs on it. "I wouldn't have brought her here if I thought she was dangerous. Besides, she needs to talk to you, too. Something's happened."

Shondra shoves the harpoon gun into Jake's chest and moves

carefully around the desk, past us, to the door. I humor her and step out of her way. "I don't want to stay in this room longer than I have to," she says to Jake, even though she's staring at me. "I'll be with Lane. Come and find me when you're done."

Jake watches her go.

"What is it?" he asks. He doesn't put the gun down. His voice is still sharp. His green eyes have turned stormy since the last time I saw him, vats of churning acid. His letter jacket is pinned to the wall behind him like the skin of another animal he hunted down and killed.

Jeffrey looks at me.

"Julie Wisnowski is dead," I say. Then, correcting myself: "Julie Wisnowski *was murdered.*"

Jake frowns. "The class president?"

.12. ...

The same night.

We braved the mosquitoes to sit on the front curb outside Jeffrey's house while we waited for my dad to pick me up.

The day's heat had finally cooled, and Jeffrey's neighborhood was lit by yellow streetlights. It was eerily quiet, except for the crickets. Jeffrey wrapped his arms around his legs and pulled his knees up to his chest so he could rest his chin on them.

I'd never seen him so down. At school he was titanium; here he was cardboard.

Sorry, he said. Jake's friends are usually jerks, I just thought they'd lay off today.

Do you always have to apologize for your family? I asked.

I guess I don't have to, but I feel like I should. I didn't

expect them to jump on you like that. I mean, I don't know about you, but I like it when we get to hang out, and I thought if both of us were together, they would ignore us. Instead it felt like I gave them more fuel.

I didn't exactly help myself with all that staring, I said.

Why did you? Do you like him?

I . . . don't know. Yes. I guess. I don't know. I turned away, face burning. Is that bad?

Jeffrey was quiet for a minute. Finally he said, A lot of girls like Jake.

I knew that. I didn't want to think about it, but I knew it. It was an inevitable thing, like people enjoying ice cream. A few people don't, but most of them do.

Jeffrey was picking at a loose piece of asphalt at his feet. That Jeffrey Blumenthal's Best Friend brand on my forehead throbbed hard.

I like it when we get to hang out, too, I said. We don't have to do anything. Just this is fine. Besides, I'm sure I won't like Jake for long. He's kind of a jerk.

Jeffrey smiled.

What are you two lovebirds doing over there?

The question came from across the street. Jeffrey and I looked up at the same time. Traipsing through the neighbor's yard and into the glow of the streetlamp was Ken Kapoor and his four friends.

Hi, Ken, Jeffrey said.

Ken grinned at us. He was a freshman, like Jake, and was one of those guys who wore his Wayfarers at night, but it was fine because he wasn't doing it to impress anyone; he just really liked his Wayfarers. Also, you really didn't want to make fun of Ken Kapoor, for anything. It wasn't worth it. The cuffs of his jeans were always turned up and he wore bright red Converse and flannel shirts with the sleeves rolled to his elbows. When he called us lovebirds, he didn't mean it in any specific way, it was just how he talked.

Ken was the kind of person you wanted. You either wanted to date him, to be his friend, or to be him, because he seemed so above it all. He wasn't one of Us. He wasn't one of Them. He knew who he was and he wasn't going to let anyone take it away from him. From down here in the river, it seemed like he'd seen the path to the sea and was just enjoying the ride. I had a crush on Ken. Everyone had a crush on Ken.

Cat Lady, is that you? Ken stopped walking and hooked a finger around his Wayfarers to pull them down and look over them. I didn't know you came scavenging in these parts.

Got invited to a party, I said, motioning back toward the house.

Ken made a strangled noise and grabbed at his shiny black hair, pretending he was dying. Oh, the football players! The cookouts! The four years of high school mediocrity! His friends chuckled. I don't know how you deal with it, Jefferson, he said to Jeffrey as he straightened up. That brother of yours is a real piece of work.

Jeffrey shrugged. What are you all doing?

Ken snapped his fingers and one of his friends held up a black duffel bag and another friend reached inside and pulled out a large yellow cheese hat. Ken took it and shoved it on his head.

A night of mischief, Ken said.

Mischief with a cheese hat? I asked.

Ken's friends laughed.

If you can't see the mischievous opportunities provided by a cheese hat, Ken said, I can't explain them to you.

We're going to trick Ryan Lancaster's mom into thinking she won a lifetime supply of cheese, said one of Ken's friends.

Dammit, Tod, Ken said.

Sorry, said Tod.

Is that a good idea? Jeffrey asked. Isn't Ryan Lancaster's mom, like, ill?

Ken shrugged. I guess you'll know if the neighborhood goes up in flames, won't you, Jefferson? It's Ryan you have to look out for anyway; he's the one with the weird YouTube channel where he sets shit on fire. Well, listen, have fun with your brother. Tell him I hope it doesn't hurt too much when the seniors shove his own ego up his ass.

Ken and his friends sauntered off, still laughing.

It didn't surprise me that some people didn't like Jake. Everyone knew Jake, and everyone either loved him or hated him, and some probably loved and hated him. But it did surprise me that Ken Kapoor hated him, because Ken didn't seem to care what anyone did enough to hate them.

I'm glad Jake's in high school now, Jeffrey said after Ken and the others were well out of earshot. It's weird, though, because I'm kind of sad about it, too.

Why? I asked.

Because he's my brother, Jeffrey said. When we were little, our dad used to say we were each other's right-hand man. And I know he's a dick, but without him I'm alone.

Maybe these particular memories are just to remind me how much I hate Jake.

THE BROTHERS BLUMENTHAL

"**Y**es," I say. "Julie Wisnowski. We think she got in a fight with someone and they cracked her head open on the pavement in the courtyard."

"Maybe she shouldn't have gotten into a fight with them, then." Jake stows the harpoon gun somewhere below the desk and pulls out a wooden baseball bat. You'd think this would be less threatening, but the baseball bat has a circular saw jammed into its tip with blades that look like shark teeth. This is the kind of weapon someone makes when they want to joke around about hurting people. Jake comes out from behind the desk, balances the teeth on the floor, leans on the bat. "Why should I care? What you weirdos get up to out there is your own problem."

"I'd say it's everyone's problem when someone gets murdered,"

I say, eyeing the bat. "We don't feel safe now." Not that we did before, but now we're getting killed in supposedly safe places like the courtyard instead of in the hallways by Laserbeams. "The sooner we can find out who did this, the sooner everything can go back to normal."

Jake scoffs. Jeffrey shuffles uneasily beside me. We all know there is no *normal*, but sometimes we have to pretend.

"Okay," Jake says. "I'm still not following. What did you come here for? We didn't do it, and if you thought we had, you wouldn't have come here. Don't tell me you expect me to send someone out to investigate? This place is a stronghold. We stay in here *because* of the assholes out there killing people. Your wanderers keep trying to pick us off."

"There's only one now," I spit. "Mark. The others disappeared. And they're not *our* wanderers. They attack us, too."

"We weren't sure if anyone here had heard anything," Jeffrey says, cutting me off before I can say more. "I know you pay the Hands for information about what's going on."

Jake's mouth twists up in a cruel smile. "If you want information, Jeffers, you should go ask Time and the Hands for it yourself."

Jeffrey visibly shudders. He has to grab the sides of his head to keep its movement from disorienting him, destroying any hope he has of keeping his reaction a secret. Asking Time and the Hands for help isn't really an option; Time always charges a steep price for his information.

"But to answer your question," Jake continues, "no, I haven't heard anything from the Hands. Though it could be because they're the ones who killed her. You never know—that Time, he's a wild card. Maybe he finally decided to try out the Big Bad Sacrifice."

The Big Bad Sacrifice is the name someone gave to the theory that eradicating the kids who have changed will let everyone else out of School. We're all such clever people here.

"I don't think Time's stupid enough to believe killing us will reveal the way out of this place," I say. I am careful not to move. Not to shift my weight, twitch my fingers, even tilt my head. Perhaps it makes me look less human, but it also makes me look less vulnerable. "But not everyone is smart like him."

Jake stares at me. His eyes begin to boil over. "What are you implying?"

Jeffrey looks at me in alarm.

I stare back at Jake. "Are we really going to pretend you don't have an issue with us? That if anyone was going to test the Big Bad Sacrifice, it wouldn't be you?"

"I think that's a bit of a strong accusation to make." Jeffrey turns to me, his head vibrating with worry. "Right, Cat? I mean, none of us would do that. Or even think of it."

"We've thought about it hard enough to name it," I say.

Jake begins spinning the baseball bat; the floor squeals softly in pain. He stares at us with that dead-eyed predator look he's always had. Before all this happened, I thought that was a sexy smolder, something he'd worked on to pick up his various girlfriends. Now I see the blankness for what it is, the lack of conscience between his ears, the dark wasteland in his head broken only by the strobing lights of instinct.

"I won't let you do this," he says finally.

"Do what?" Jeffrey asks, his voice weak.

"Let you pin the blame on us to divert attention away from yourselves."

"You can't be serious," I say. "We didn't blame it on you. We came for *help*."

"Serious as a heart attack," says Jake. He jerks his chin toward the door. "They'll believe me, if I say it. It doesn't matter if it's true. You may think I'm the only one who hates you here—"

I can't help the snort.

"—but no one would bat an eyelash if I decided to cancel our truce."

"You can't do that!" Jeffrey takes a step closer to Jake, and Jake steps back, dragging the bat's saw blade against the floor. Jeffrey doesn't seem to notice. He holds his hands out. "Please, Jake, don't do it. You don't have to help us. We'll leave, okay? We'll figure it out on our own. If . . . if you cancel the truce, that could start a war. We don't—that's not—it won't help anyone stay alive."

A muscle clenches in Jake's jaw. "Jesus, Jeffrey. I can't believe you're my brother. You're pitiful."

Jeffrey flinches. "I think there's a better way—"

"Than what we have right now?" Jake asks, his voice getting louder. "Than no one getting out and nothing ever changing, except your freaky faces? Yeah, there is. And if it means you all die, I'm not going to stop it from happening."

Jeffrey takes a step closer to his brother. Jake backs up behind the desk, raising his saw-blade bat. I grab Jeffrey's arm to reel him back, but there's no need. The bat isn't meant for him.

"Remember that thing Dad used to say?" Jake asks Jeffrey. "When we were little, before he left us? That we should always be there for each other?"

"Right-hand men," Jeffrey says.

"That," Jake says.

Then he slams his right hand flat on the desk, and with his left hand brings the saw blade down with such astounding force it slices clean through his wrist.

. 13. . . .

The crack of the bat through bone.

Eighth grade.

We were the oldest kids in the middle school, and most everyone who had made things hard for us before—the Lanes, the Raphs—had moved on to high school. Some were still there, but they were easy to ignore. I had Jeffrey, who was growing too quickly for his clothes to keep up, and my art, which still didn't include flowers. I had my mom, who let me help with her newest gallery exhibit, and Dad, who paid me to help him organize his finance work.

My life that year was a long, soothing string of white noise, familiar and unbroken.

Except for those times when I went to Jeffrey's house, and Jake was there.

Then the cymbals crashed and drums exploded and trumpets blasted in my ears until I couldn't talk or think or even move properly. It felt like someone had shoved oiled ball joints into my sockets and my limbs were flapping around in every direction, heedless of where I told them to go.

One time we walked into Jeffrey's kitchen and Jake was at the table with his homework, and he looked up and said, Hey, Cracks McGee, to Jeffrey, and before Jeffrey had a chance to respond in his breaking voice, Jake looked at me and said, *Heeeere, kitty cat.*

My face lit up like a firecracker. I stood in the doorway while Jeffrey asked Jake not to call me *kitty cat* and retrieved two cans of root beer from the fridge and a large bag of Skittles from the pantry. Jake ignored him and went back to his homework.

The cymbals and drums and trumpets in my heart beat too hard against my ribs all the way back to Jeffrey's room, where we played video games and got a sugar rush from the root beer and Skittles and made each other giggle until later that night when my dad finally came to get me. I didn't know what Jake *was*, exactly, or why my body rebelled so harshly against me when he was around, but I knew I needed him the way I needed sunlight. It hurt, knowing he was there, but

I couldn't touch him, couldn't speak to him, as if we were on two sides of a thick glass wall.

Eighth grade wasn't so bad, because I only saw Jake sometimes. Jeffrey talked about him occasionally—less and less as the year went on—and a few days after seeing Jake, the white noise always settled down, and everything returned to the way it was supposed to be.

In eighth grade I didn't have to deal with all the other girls who liked Jake. I didn't have to see him every day. I was okay with thinking about him from afar, sitting in English class and daydreaming about what it would be like to date him, what it would be like if he didn't make fun of me. It eased the ache, if only for a little while.

CRACK

I have seen more blood today than I ever want to see again.

The desk is coated with it. So is the bat. And the rest of Jake's arm, and his face. It drips in syrupy rivulets to the floor.

I don't know what to do. It's everywhere.

A moment after Jake slices off his own right hand, he tosses the baseball bat at Jeffrey's feet and screams for Raph.

Raph nearly knocks the door down. I grab Jeffrey and we're running, shoving Raph out of the way, sprinting down the long hallway, past the smoky rooms and the violent games. When we reach the door, a crossbow bolt slams into the wood next to my head. I yank Jeffrey through.

"They won't follow us here." I repeat it over and over, yelling at first, then softer and softer, until we're far away from administration.

School is quiet. We've been too loud.

Jeffrey lets me pull him like a paper doll, no matter what direction I turn, even when I get a little lost. After several minutes of this, I realize how heavy his hand is in mine. Now he's more like a bag of cement. I stop in the middle of a hallway, against a tall, dark row of lockers, long abandoned by their owners. Jeffrey hesitates for a moment, face frozen and eyes fixed on his feet, then slumps against the lockers and slides to the floor. Tiny dark spots of blood have begun to dry on the front of his sweater vest. I kneel in front of him. There's a small fleck of blood near the corner of his face that I want to wipe away, but I have no way to wet my fingers.

I see the moment Jake sliced into his wrist over and over, like a rotating image in my head. I already know it will be in there forever. Violence leaves scars.

"They won't all believe him," I say. Quietly, though nothing seems quiet enough for these dark hallways. "Not everyone in administration is like Jake. And we can keep the others out here safe. We can keep them in the Fountain Room, and they can always stay with a friend. It doesn't have to come down to a fight. They won't leave administration, and we don't have to make them."

Jeffrey's eyes squeeze into pained lines. His mouth can never close, the same way mine can never open, and now the downturned corners and the square teeth give him that anxious, frightened look he wears far too often. He holds the sides of his head, like he's trying to squeeze it back into its old shape.

"Jeffrey," I say. I grab his forearms but don't try to pry his hands away.

"Why did he do that?" he says. "Why did he throw the bat at me? Why did he make it look like I did it?"

I say nothing.

"I didn't want that," he says. "Why did he just cut it off like that? I didn't want him to, I didn't mean to make him mad, I didn't know he'd think we were accusing him—"

"*Jeffrey*," I say. His eyes become circles again when he looks at me. "I'm sorry."

He finally lowers his hands.

"I have to go talk to him," he says, grabbing the locker dials to pull himself up. "He'll still listen to me—I can still be useful to him—he'll listen." Jeffrey starts walking. I grab his arm and the back of his sweater vest to slow him down.

"You can't. *Jeffrey*, you can't! He did that—he made it look like you did that to him—to make sure they'll never let us into administration again. As soon as Raph sees you, he'll put a crossbow bolt through your head. Come *here*." I yank him back, only to see the hurt on his face, the strangely constructed, crayon-drawn hurt.

Then he looks over my shoulder, and his expression morphs gently into surprised panic.

"It's Mark," he whispers.

As slowly as I can, I look behind me. Standing shrouded in the vast darkness at the far end of the hallway is Mark. I haven't seen him in a long time. He played games in the Fountain Room, when we had them. But then he stopped talking. He left the Fountain Room and didn't come back.

Puke-yellow fur covers his body. His snout hangs open in a lopsided smile and one of his ears is missing. Grease stains his round white belly. He looks like he should be dancing for kids at a pizzeria, but instead he's been thrown to the wolves in School's hallways.

"If we look away, he'll go," Jeffrey says.

I nod. When Mark stopped talking, he started operating like all the lost students operate; he wanders the hallways by himself, no longer even attempting to communicate with the rest of us, and if you see him, you need to look in another direction. Give him permission to leave. He does not want you to stare. If you stare, he will attack.

Slowly, Jeffrey and I turn away. I'm still holding Jeffrey's wrist, squeezing as tightly as I can.

clack clack clack clack clack

I whip around and find Mark closer than before. His bulging white eyes stare straight at me, emotionless, empty. He approached faster than I thought he could, but he stands perfectly still now. Maybe I was wrong. Maybe not all of the lost operate the same way. I'm suddenly having trouble even remembering what other lost students I've encountered.

"We need to go," Jeffrey says.

I refuse to take my eyes off Mark.

"Now."

"Where?" I whisper. "He's blocking our way to the Fountain Room."

"Where do you go?" he asks. "Your place. You always come from the other direction."

The boiler room. It has been my spot for as long as I've been here, and I've been careful to keep everyone out of it, including Jeffrey. But I don't know what demon has wormed its way into Mark, and I don't plan on letting Jeffrey stay here to find out.

"We'll have to run," I say.

.14. ...

Freshman orientation.

End of the summer.

Jeffrey and I sat in the middle of the auditorium.

The athletic director was onstage explaining to us why we should go out for sports. A lot of the faces in the crowd were familiar to me, faces I knew from middle school, from the river. Plenty of others weren't familiar at all. Our high school was big and pulled from a lot of middle schools. I spotted Sissy and Julie together with other girls I recognized, diligently taking notes. A few rows up from them was Ryan Lancaster, hiding in the shadows at the top of the auditorium, writing something in a giant three-ring binder and slowly turning his head back and forth like a security camera surveilling the crowd. I slouched down in my seat to avoid his notice.

Jeffrey slouched down as well and leaned toward me to ask, Do I have something on my face?

No, I said. Why?

Because those girls keep looking at me and laughing.

I glanced past him and saw the girls in question. I didn't know them, but they looked fairly standard.

I think it's because you're wearing a sweater vest, I said.

Jeffrey flattened his hands over his new charcoal sweater vest.

But I like my sweater vest, he said.

The girls probably thought he was some kind of loser. But anything Jeffrey wore, he wore so earnestly it was impossible to make fun of the way he dressed. These girls must not have gotten the memo.

Want me to go make them stop? I asked.

I didn't think anything I said to them would actually do any good. With my luck they'd start making fun of me, the weird girl with the eyes looking different directions, wearing a black turtleneck in August. In my defense, the fabric was light and I knew we'd be in air-conditioning all day. I doubted they'd care about that, though.

No, Jeffrey said after a second. It's fine, I just don't get it. What's not to get?

What's in it for them? Hey, look at the kid wearing the sweater vest, isn't that so weird that he's wearing a sweater vest, how out of touch is he, let's laugh about it, ha ha ha. Like, why do they care that I'm wearing a sweater vest? Is the sweater vest attacking them?

I like your sweater vest, I said.

He turned back to me and smiled, his storm cloud dissipating. Jeffrey didn't normally have storm clouds—usually they only formed when he was frustrated about something with Jake or his mom—but when he did, it was best to shoo them away as fast as possible.

It helped, too, that a second after I told him I liked his sweater vest, a large boy tripped up the auditorium steps, and the girls broke into another loud round of giggles. The boy who'd tripped grabbed the aisle railing to pull himself back onto his thick legs. His skin was splotchy with color. He wore fraying jean shorts and socks of that special color that only occurs when something white has been worn too often.

The boy shuffled up the stairs and slid into one of the empty seats behind me and Jeffrey. The smell washed over us: a foul aroma of unwashed clothing and stale junk food that made me lose my train of thought. I stopped myself from pulling my turtleneck up over my nose.

Hey.

The boy leaned down between us. The smell turned putrid. Unwashed armpits.

Have they said anything important? I was in the bathroom.

No, Jeffrey replied with a tight smile. Still talking about sports.

Oh, good. Thanks.

The boy leaned back. I sucked in a quick breath. He leaned forward again.

I'm Mark, he said.

Jeffrey, said Jeffrey. His face began to change color from lack of oxygen.

Cat, I said.

Meow, said Mark.

I was willing to give Mark the benefit of the doubt until that. I gave Jeffrey my very best *I do not like this person* glance as I turned back around, but Jeffrey had already gotten the message.

Nice to meet you, Jeffrey said, and promptly faced forward.

Mark was quiet for a second, then retreated to his seat. A little ball of guilt gathered behind my sternum.

The lectures lasted for another hour—Mark didn't try to talk to us again, and the girls across the aisle stopped giggling—and then we went to lunch. Only freshmen had orientation today; all the other high schoolers were on their normal first day of school, and when we filed into the cafeteria, there they were. Jeffrey and I made it into the first lunch rotation. We huddled together in line for macaroni.

This place is huge, Jeffrey said, glancing up at the high ceiling and around at the hundreds of round tables. His eyes stopped on the pair of basketball players in front of us, who together had to be at least twelve and a half feet tall.

We'll get used to it, I said, mostly for my own benefit. Jeffrey was by far the taller of the two of us, and still shooting up like a weed. If everything here seemed huge to him, I was in the land of giants. A pair of senior girls cut us in line without even seeming to realize we were there. Jeffrey started to tap one of them on the shoulder, and I stopped him.

Leave it, I said.

He stuffed his hands in his pockets.

Eventually we got our macaroni and went out to find a table. It was a sea of heads with no dry land in sight.

Maybe Jake's in here somewhere, Jeffrey said.

My stomach tripped down a few steps. I'd been keeping myself from thinking about Jake all day. All week. Part of my body said, *Yes yes sit with Jake* and the other part said, *No no he'll find out you like him.*

There has to be an empty spot, I said, standing on tiptoe and craning my neck. Absolutely nothing. How was this possible?

Jefferson and the Cat Lady!

We turned at the same time and found Ken Kapoor, flanked by friends, lounging at a nearby table with his feet kicked up. He jerked his chin at us and smiled. High school hadn't dulled Ken's luster as it did so many kids'; it had put a sheen on him. He was the king of his own small kingdom, and his people were safe—if a little oppressed—under his confident hand. It would have been nice to be included under that reign, but I didn't know if safety was worth the price Ken exacted from the people closest to him. They never seemed to make any decisions for themselves; they just did what Ken said.

How's it going, kids? he asked.

Is the cafeteria always this full? I said.

Pretty much. You can have this table—we're about to leave.

Jeffrey and I set our trays down, but neither of us pulled out a chair. Ken was still staring at us, eyes hidden behind his Wayfarers, like he expected one of us to burst into song. He managed to look like a senior while actually being a sophomore.

So, Ken said, heard you're friends with Chubby Mark now.

Chubby Mark? Jeffrey asked.

Please, Jeffers, you know who I'm talking about. Chubby Kevin's little brother is a freshman this year, and I have it on good authority that he was sitting with you two at orientation. The whole family goes to Chubby Cheese's every night, eats nothing but stale pizza and breadsticks. Jesus, Chubby Kevin is the guy *inside* the Chubby Cheese suit. How do you not know this?

He wasn't sitting with us, I said, a little startled at how quickly it came out.

One of Ken's eyebrows shot up. Is that so? he said. Well, let me give you a warning: Chubby Kevin is advised to take a bath at least twice a day—by *teachers*, mind you—and I'm assuming his brother will fare no better. Watch out for that kid; he's a fly.

A fly? I said.

Yeah. He's a fly and you two are some sweet, ripe fruit. You're asking for a little creep to start following you around, trying to be your friend. He'll worm his way into all your jokes, invite himself to your parties, show up at your house when you never even gave him your address.

Jeffrey looked at me, then back at Ken. Has that happened to you?

Yeah, thanks to goddamn Ryan Lancaster! Ken said. Where have you two been for the past three years? Down in your fucking sad-painting-sweater-vest hidey-hole? The asshole tried to tear my goddamn hair out when I told him we weren't friends. Said he put me on *a list*, like he's some kind of supervillain. Got him back about a thousand times over for that one. So let me tell you—don't let it come down to that, kids! Cut Chubby Mark off before he gets started!

I silently wished Ken and his friends would leave.

Thanks for the advice, Jeffrey said, not sounding very thankful at all.

Ken dropped his feet from the table and stood. You're not gonna be so flippant when you realize I'm right, he said, and walked off. His friends gathered up their bags and followed him.

Jeffrey and I took our seats.

Jeffrey sighed.

Yeah, I know, I said.

Someone at the next table snorted and gestured. I looked up and saw Mark, tripping his way out of the line, heading to an empty table by the windows. He looked around as he walked, like everyone else, trying to find someone to sit with.

Jeffrey was watching him, too.

Should we? he asked.

I watched Mark sit down. Watched him start eating his macaroni. Hunched over as he was, his sweat-stained shirt had hiked up to reveal an unfortunate patch of hair. I knew we shouldn't call him Chubby Mark. I knew being fat wasn't a bad thing, and I shouldn't make fun of him for that or for anything else.

I also knew you were only as safe as you made yourself, and being nice to Mark had already proved unsafe.

So I said, No, we shouldn't.

And we didn't.

BOILER

Mark's footsteps clip after us at an alarming pace. He seems faster than he should be with that unwieldy body. Every time I look over my shoulder, he is there. Twenty-five feet. Twenty feet. Twenty-five.

I hold myself back so Jeffrey doesn't fall behind, though I want to run faster; I want to push myself as fast as I can go, because I know I can outrun Mark. I don't get tired, and I never trip. Jeffrey was breathing hard after the sprint away from administration, and now his stride is breaking, loose and straggly.

We reach the staircase to the boiler room, hidden between the cafeteria and the gym, much sooner than we should. I suspect School shifted it closer to help us. I rip the door open and shove Jeffrey through, then dive in and slam the door shut behind me, throwing the lock. When I look through the narrow rectangular window above the door handle, I see a bulging white eye and half a matted yellow face. Mark's bear-mouse-dog snout taps against the windowpane.

"Go!" I tell Jeffrey. "Down!"

The handle rattles. The door remains firmly shut.

I turn and follow Jeffrey down the stairs. The stairwell is lit by a small red light at the very bottom. Jeffrey waits there for me, head tipped up, focused on the rattling.

"Ignore it," I say, stepping past him to open the door. "He'll go away."

"He's never acted like that before," Jeffrey says.

"He's never been that changed before," I reply.

Like the courtyard, the boiler room does not shift with School's inhaling and exhaling. It's always the same, a cavernous space made of steel and fire. Taking up most of the room is School's heart, the boiler whose pipes root their way up and tear into the ceiling and the walls, like the boiler itself is holding the school together. It radiates an orange-red glow from the teeth-like grates in its front. It's warm here, but never hot. Not to me.

Jeffrey stares at the boiler with the same trepidation I had when I first arrived.

"You sleep here?" he asks.

I lead him through the pipes. Behind, nestled between the arteries, is a small nook lined by blankets and pillows. I settle in and pat the space next to me. This little nest was already set up, the first time I came here, like someone had slept in it before me. I had been guided here by instinct, by muscle memory. It could have been me who was sleeping here, and I didn't remember.

"We'll be safe," I say. "Until Mark leaves. Then we can go back to the Fountain Room and tell the others what happened."

Jeffrey climbs in and pulls his legs up to his chest. His face has that faded, weatherworn look it gets whenever he's tired. He rubs his right wrist like he's missing a watch he usually wears. I want to embrace him, to help him, but I don't know how. I have the sick feeling that I *did* know, once, and the problem now isn't that I've forgotten, but that I'm no longer allowed.

"Hey," I say. "Remember the time you had to stay after school for that speech team meeting, and I hung back to finish a painting, and by the time we were both done, the whole school was deserted and we walked around?"

I seem to be remembering an awful lot today, and that particular memory comes to me as I say it. Jeffrey frowns, scratching the side of his head.

"No, not really . . . " he says. His frown deepens. "But . . . it seems familiar. Isn't that weird? I don't remember it at all, but I know you're right."

"How much do you remember?"

"Some things. I remember everyone—most everyone. But there used to be more people. A lot more. I remember knowing everyone who's here, but . . . like, Mark. I don't remember Mark's last name, but I know that mascot thing is Mark. I know that Julie was class president. I know we're"—his hesitation lasts only a second—"best friends. And I know Jake is—Jake was—"

A shudder wracks his body, and he grabs his head. He lowers it, resting it on his knees.

"Why don't you lie down?" I say after several moments. "A lot has happened."

I have to nudge his arm to get him started, but he eventually shifts over and lies down on his back—the only way he *can* because of his head—and curls his legs up so he fits between the pipes. He stares at the ceiling for a while, until he closes his eyes.

I sit beside him, one hand still resting on his arm. He takes it in his, squeezes my fingers.

I'm too angry with Jake to be disturbed by what he did. He hates all of us for being different, for being changed and strange, and then he goes and does it to himself and calls it righteous. Severing himself from his own brother.

Eventually I stretch out beside Jeffrey and fall asleep.

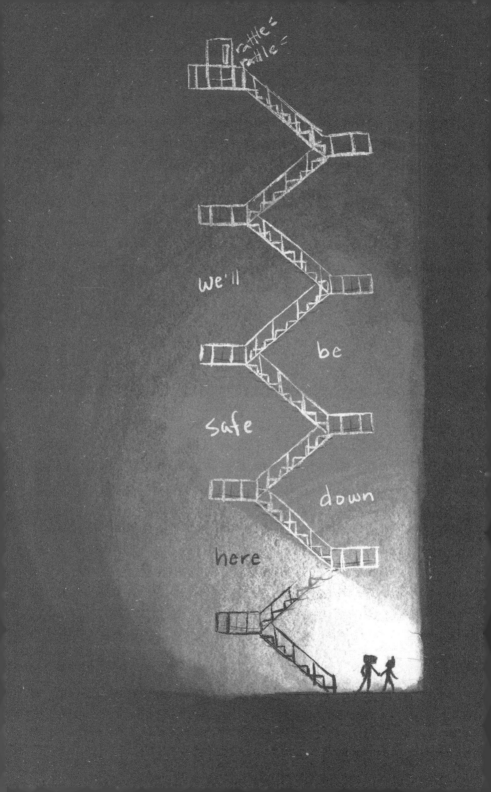

. 15. ...

Too many of us.

The river of freshman year faces had become whitewater rapids, and the current battered me constantly, pulling me under until Jeffrey came along and yanked my head above the surface. My parents had gotten me a phone, so we could text even when we weren't in class together, and that helped me more than once.

We took Ken Kapoor's lunch table every day after he and his friends left. A week into the year, we were joined by Sissy and Julie, who had been Krazy Glued together after eighth grade. Over the summer Sissy had attempted to tame her mane of frizzy hair by cutting it nearly down to her scalp, but now a group of juniors called her "The Butcher" every time they saw her, and Sissy had invested in a wide variety of hoodies and cute hats.

Now they talk about my eczema all the time, Sissy said on tomato soup day, yanking her sleeve farther down over her right arm, the one that had always looked a little red and bubbly, reminding me weirdly of an octopus. It's, like, have you never seen chronic skin inflammation before?

They're jerks, Julie said, glancing over her shoulder. As far as I knew, she hadn't cried because of a bad grade yet. But she had teared up a little in geometry after we got our first partner test back and she discovered that neither she nor her partner had any idea how to find the degree of an angle.

Mark left the lunch line and looked our way for a second before moving on to the table by the windows by himself.

How has your first week been, Cat? Sissy asked, tugging her beanie farther down around her ears.

Fine, I said. In truth, it had been horrible. Every day I looked forward to three o'clock. I had to ride the bus home, but at least it was home. I helped Dad for a while, then it was dinnertime, then homework, and then I had enough time before bed to do a few sketches. Teachers as inanimate objects or animals or natural formations, because that's sometimes what they felt like to me, there to serve a purpose and unable to see me. Images of dark hallways and impossibly tall doors, or tight spaces with a hand reaching through, as if trapped. More than one of my drawings were stylized renditions of a boy with dark hair and green eyes, smiling at me, or with his head tipped toward the sun.

I didn't dare bring my sketchbooks to school. And my doodles stayed safe and small in the margins of my class notes, and I didn't let anyone see them.

Out of nowhere, Jeffrey was shoved forward so violently his nose plunged into his tomato soup. He yelped and came up snorting and spluttering. Jake strolled past with a few older boys.

Hey, Jeff, he said. You have something on your nose.

The older boys laughed as they walked away, and Jeffrey, eyes tearing up from the hot soup, swiped his napkin over his face. I had to clap my hand over my mouth to keep from giggling. Jeffrey shot me a look, unamused, his nose bright red. My laughter died, and shame swept in.

Are you okay? Sissy asked.

I'm fine, Jeffrey said, his voice cracking, but thank you for asking.

He gave her his soothing smile, the little quirk of the lips that could set anyone's worries at ease. But it was different than it used to be. It was like his face was being torn slowly from the muscles beneath it—he was still himself and his expressions were still his expressions, but his face didn't fit them the way it used to. My parents would have said it was just puberty, but it didn't feel that way to me. It felt like his body was changing to fit something new inside.

When I went home that night, I opened the sketchbook sitting on my dresser, and flipped to the back. There was the green-eyed boy smiling at me. My heart thudded painfully in my chest. I constantly reminded myself I couldn't lose Jake if I'd never had him, but that was how it felt.

That part of me, the painful hollow behind my ribs, couldn't fathom him doing what he'd been doing to Jeffrey lately. At their house, when Jake was there without his friends, they kind of acted like brothers. True, Jake sometimes paid more attention to the giant Saint Bernards than he did to Jeffrey, but it wasn't like at school. At school, Jake was charismatic and funny and talented, and he made the people he cared about feel like they were special. And at school, Jeffrey became *Jake Blumenthal's Loser Brother.* Which was weird, because Jeffrey was the friendliest and kindest person I knew. Jeffrey shut down bullies with a *smile.* Jeffrey could talk to anyone, about anything. He was as charismatic as Jake, but he cared about everyone, not just the people he thought were worthy of it. Why would Jake go along with everyone else, making fun of his brother? Why would Jake treat Jeffrey like that?

It was that night, staring at my sketchbook, that I first considered that maybe Jake hadn't gone along with everyone else.

Maybe everyone else had gone along with Jake.

DREAMLESS

I can speak to School. That doesn't always mean School speaks back. Asleep behind the boiler, I float in the darkness in my head, with my memories and my anger, and I ask *Why are all the doors gone?* and *When will we be allowed to leave?* and *Why are we changing?* and *What happens to the lost students?*

School never answers.

School doesn't mind answering questions like *How are you feeling today?* and *What's your favorite color?* Answers: Blue; red.

Tonight, or today, whichever is more correct since it's impossible to gauge time or days here, I feel School, somewhere. Not physically, but like a voice humming a tune, walking circles around me, sometimes closer and sometimes farther away. With all my usual questions asked and unanswered, I ask one more,

Who killed Julie Wisnowski? and School gives a sigh that I take as a shrug. Not a shrug of ignorance, because School knows everything, but a shrug of impatience, because it knows that I know it won't answer, and I go on asking anyway.

I don't know what else to say. In all the time we've been here, which feels like forever and yet I can't pinpoint when it all started, my questions have drained away with my curiosity. I have so little left.

I ask, *Is Jeffrey dreaming?*

School says, *Yes.*

I ask, *What about?*

School says, *Would you like to see?*

I pause. I shouldn't intrude on Jeffrey's dreams—I already have a good idea what they'll be about, anyway—but maybe if I know what's happening in his head, I'll be able to help him when he wakes up.

I say, *Okay.*

The darkness around me fills with light. I'm standing in Jake's cave office, but it's far too bright, the way School's hallways get bright when it exhales and they constrict. Jake stands behind his desk with his hand flat on the desktop and his sawtooth bat raised above his head. Jeffrey stands in front of the desk, and he doesn't have his rectangular cardboard head but instead looks the way he used to, except too pale, like he's slowly fading out of the world. I'm there, too, standing behind Jeffrey, and even though I don't have my cat mask, my face is a blank slate, no eyes or nose or mouth, and I don't move.

The scene unfolds in slow motion. Jeffrey reaches out to stop Jake, but Jake is faster. The saw comes down and rips through Jake's wrist, fountaining blood and splintering bone. Black tendrils lash up Jake's arm from his wrist, turning his skin the color of a starless night sky. They cover him, devouring him, wrapping around his neck and head like vines. His eyes glow green, and a scream of anger rips from his chest.

Jeffrey is a white outline cowering in fear as his brother looms over him. Jake's severed hand flops off the desk and bursts into a thousand blue chrysanthemum petals that wither and blacken as soon as they touch the floor.

The dream whips away, a rubber band pulled until it snaps. School hums its tune around me again.

I ask, *Can you make his dreams better?*

School says, *No.*

.16. ....

April of freshman year.

Jeffrey came over to my house for the first time.

Like everyone, he marveled at the nursery my parents ran in the shop attached to our house and the small army of bonsai Mom had been growing for years. The little trees sat everywhere, underneath plant lights, on trays outside the windows, filling the back deck. It had always been strange to me to go to someone else's house and see no plants; it was comforting to know that someone else could come to my house and find it just as strange to see so many.

Mom was clearly pleased with Jeffrey's appreciation of her work, even if her modesty wouldn't let her show it. It took a fair bit of time to pry him away from her, but I finally escaped with him upstairs.

This is your room? He stood on the threshold and looked around.

Yep, I said.

Your name is on the wall. He pointed to the letters painted above my bed in gold and blue. In this memory they are smeared, unreadable.

My mom did it when I was born, I said.

I flopped over on the bed and watched Jeffrey pad across the room in his socks. He examined the paintings and drawings pinned to the walls. Brushed his hands over the little jade tree on the dresser. The trunk of the tree twisted at nearly a ninety-degree angle, its branches hardly longer than a finger, the small round leaves carefully shaped into clusters.

Did you grow this one? he asked.

I shook my head. Mom did.

He kept exploring. He was too gangly for this room, for my whole house, but as always he kept himself carefully contained. Like his entire mission on Earth was to make sure he never left a trace. I had to mark everything, even if no one ever saw. I had to draw picture after picture, and it never felt like enough. I was pretty sure when I died, I would still feel like I hadn't been here, like I hadn't done anything that someone would remember me for. I was just some high school girl with paint on her hands and a house full of trees.

Wow, Cat—you should do flowers more often, Jeffrey said. He had found my sketchbook and turned it toward me. It was open to a colored pencil sketch of a blue chrysanthemum.

I had done that one because Jeffrey's mom kept chrysanthemums on their front porch. Red and yellow and white, but no blue, because chrysanthemums weren't naturally blue. If I was going to draw a flower, it had to be at least a little different. It had to be weird.

Maybe, I said, knowing I didn't mean it.

I didn't realize the sketchbook Jeffrey had picked up was *the* sketchbook. I didn't realize I'd left it on top of the stack on my nightstand.

He flipped the page and froze.

Wait! I sat up, reaching for the book. Jeffrey stared at the picture, expressionless.

You know, he said, I bet Jake would be pretty flattered that you drew him.

Please don't tell him, I said. Promise me you won't tell him.

I crawled across the bed and grabbed the sketchbook and held it to my chest.

Jeffrey's hands hovered in the air for a moment before

he carefully tucked them into his pockets. His eyebrows furrowed.

I won't tell him, he said.

I slid the sketchbook into my nightstand drawer.

After a minute of thick silence, Jeffrey said, Why didn't you tell me?

That I drew a picture of him? Sorry, I didn't know you were the art police.

That's not what I meant.

You already knew. I told you forever ago, at that party.

Yeah, but you said you'd get over him. If you're going to have a crush on my brother for two whole years, I'd like to know about it.

I don't have a crush on him.

Cat!

I recoiled. Jeffrey never raised his voice.

Why does it matter? I asked.

Because you come over to my house, he said. Because you hang out with me. Is that just because of him?

No!

He didn't seem convinced.

Jeffrey Blumenthal's Best Friend.

We're best friends, I said. Jake doesn't matter. We should be . . . should be eating pizza sticks and Skittles and . . . laughing at bad horror movies. And your dogs can be there slobbering all over us, and it'll be great, like always. Can we do that?

He glanced at the nightstand drawer.

Jake doesn't matter? he said.

Jake doesn't matter, I said. Not between us.

HANDGUARDS

Jeffrey is gone.

The room shifts. I crawl out from under the pipes and find the rest of the boiler room vacant. I carefully climb up the stairs and listen at the door. The hallway is quiet.

Jeffrey left, which must mean Mark is gone. I tread carefully anyway, because the hallways are vast and dark at present, and I know Mark is adept at hiding in the shadows. Bubbles of anxiety begin to form in my stomach as events rush back to me.

I need to tell everyone what happened.

I need to warn them.

I need to find out who attacked Julie, and why, and how I can stop them from attacking again.

I need to make sure Jeffrey is okay.

My first stop is the Fountain Room. Like administration, it's a gathering place, but for the ones like me. Changed ones who haven't lost themselves and started roaming the halls. The Fountain Room definitely didn't exist before. It sits a little past the courtyard where Julie was killed. There are four doors, one in each wall, all of them wide open.

We named the room because of the two large fountains at each end. They would look less out of place in a city square, surrounded by skyscrapers and endless droves of pedestrians. Here they are giant crystal pools that flood when School exhales and the walls close in. When School inhales and the walls and ceiling are far away, the fountain jets shoot clear up into the darkness.

Between the two fountains is a small commune of blankets, pillows, lanterns, tarps, tents, backpacks, books and notebooks, assorted foods for those of us who can eat, and anything else we've been able to scrounge. Several students sit in a small circle there, including Sissy, who is wrapped in a large fleece blanket patterned with hundreds of sheep jumping over fences. She looks small today, like a bug stuck on a windshield. Her back is to me, but the others see me approaching and immediately freeze.

"Has Jeffrey been here?" I ask. Sissy jumps and looks up at me, her tentacle frantically twitching. No one says anything, and I remember that I no longer have eyes. I resist the urge to stick my fingers in my eyeholes, just to point out to them that I know how I look. Even they, who understand that changing doesn't always mean you're dangerous, are scared of me.

Finally West says, "No, we haven't seen him since the courtyard."

"What happened in administration?" Sissy asks.

This would be much easier if Jeffrey was with me. Jeffrey knows how to phrase things so that no one gets the wrong idea and panics.

"We went in to see if Jake or anyone else there had information about what happened to Julie," I say, making sure to look at all of them. "Either they didn't know, or they weren't telling us. Instead, Jake said we attacked him and got us run out of the offices. It was bad."

"What does that mean?" Sissy says.

"It means we can't go to administration anymore," I say. "Not even Jeffrey. Jake hates us, and I think this time he's going to be able to convince the others that we're out to get them. I don't know if they'll come out of their fortress to do anything about it, though. We'll have to watch our backs."

They nod, mute. They continue staring; I wish they would *stop staring*. Why do they look at me like I know anything? Like I have the answers?

"Tell everyone else," I say. "Tell them not to panic, but to stay vigilant. I'm going to do some investigating about what happened to Julie." My mind snaps to the courtyard. "What did we . . . I mean, her body . . . "

Sissy visibly shudders. "I was going to stay with her until we figured out what to do, but we heard another scream out in the hallway. We went to investigate, only for a *second*, and when we came back, we—she was—"

"She was gone," El says.

"Gone? Completely?"

They nod. I don't bother asking if they know who did it. If Sissy had any idea, she would have told me immediately. Besides, it might not even be one of us, changed or unchanged. It could easily be the School itself.

"If Jeffrey comes by here, tell him I'm looking for him."

I head for the north door of the Fountain Room. I shouldn't be wandering the halls alone. I'm no less susceptible to Julie's murderer or a roamer like Mark than anyone else. But I know, first, that Sissy and the others wouldn't agree to come with me even if I asked, and second, that I wouldn't want them to. I'm faster without them, and if we had to run, I couldn't leave anyone behind. I'm not Jake; I don't use bait.

I need to find Jeffrey.

School's hallways have stalled at their expanded size, the usual peak of inhaling, which means soon they'll begin compressing. I keep low to the ground, against the wall. The lockers are twelve feet tall. My ears—my facefleshhardenedstupidmaskears—stay alert as I go.

Quiet, quiet, quiet—

Click click

I pause. Listen. The noise doesn't happen again.

I continue on.

Mark will be easy to hear, with all his shoe clacking, but there's at least one other roamer I'm not sure I'd be able to fight if he snuck up on me. I know Laserbeams exists, but I don't know what he looks like. He could be anything. Anyone.

At the main hallway junction, before I can even see the front desk of administration, I stop and fade into the shadows. Administration is no longer only guarded by spike walls, but by four student guards as well, including Raph, wielding crossbows, spears, even a rusty sword. They're calm, a little lax. If Jeffrey had come here, wouldn't they be more riled up? More on edge? Or maybe they've let their guard down because they've already captured him. I don't doubt Jake would keep his brother as a hostage.

The row of lockers runs toward administration. The tops are wide and cloaked in darkness.

I squat, then leap. I swing myself up on top of the lockers without a sound, and the darkness swaddles me like a blanket. I balance there, on my haunches. Silent. I am a cat.

Carefully, quietly, I crawl toward administration. When I'm closer, I lay on my stomach and wiggle forward.

where are you?

The lockers are so wide I can't see Raph and the other guy, but I can see the heads of the boy and the girl in the middle of the hall. The girl has a crossbow like Raph's; if she sees me and has any ounce of aim, I'm getting a bolt through the eye.

Eyehole.

Whatever.

"Why are we still out here?" the boy whines. "It's creepy. Can't the next shift come out?"

"Next shift isn't due for an hour," Raph says. He's saying *hour* because he's guessing that's how long it'll be. None of us can tell time here. No clocks are the same. There is no sunlight. "Suck it up."

"Why doesn't Jake come out and do this if he's so worried about the freaks attacking us?" The girl—who I now recognize as Lane Castillo, Shondra Huston's best friend—turns her back to the hallway and puts a hand on her hip. "He always makes us do shit for him. I had a game to play!"

"Jake has you do shit for him because he's got even more shit to do on top of that," Raph barks. "Watch the hallway!"

With a huff, Lane turns away, muttering, "He'd probably get it done faster if he had two hands."

A chill runs up my spine. I pull myself closer to the edge of the lockers and peer down to get a view of Raph and the entrance. There's the front desk, and Mrs. Gearing sitting on the corner, a paper jam error flashing on her screen. The spike barricades, the other students. Raph, looking like a dick.

Then I see it: Jake's bloody hand nailed to the door behind the desk.

A warning.

I sink back into the shadows. This is no place for the changed.

"No one's ever going to come down here anyway," says the whiny boy who I think was on the football team. "We've been standing here for *hours*. It's been crickets since Blockhead and the Cat left. They're scared of us."

"As soon as we turn our backs, they'll be back," Raph says. "Shut *up* and watch *the damn hallway.*"

They do as they're told, but not without a few more muttered curses. The knots in my stomach loosen. It's clear that no one's been here since Jeffrey and I left. Even more carefully than I came, I shimmy back until it's safe to rise onto my hands and toes. I scamper to the end of the locker row and lower myself to the floor.

Jeffrey's not here.

The courtyard.

I'm halfway there, sprinting, when I trip on something in the darkness and skid five feet down the hall. I scramble up and look back. Sprawled across the floor is a large, round body. Tufts of matted fur line its silhouette. I tripped over a limb ripped from its socket, something sharp exposed at one end.

The body's single bulging eyeball gleams in the dim light. The nauseating smell of pizza grease, old cheese, and unwashed clothing fills the air.

Mark is dead.

*H*eeeeeere, kitty cat!

Sophomore year.

Jake and his football buddies whistled at me as they passed my table at the extracurriculars fair.

Over the summer, Jake took to literal catcalling every time he saw me at their house. By August it had stopped making me blush, and just made me confused.

Why was he doing it?

Why did he smile at me when he did?

Why didn't he say anything else?

Was he trying to bait me?

Did he want *me* to say something?

To do something?

I froze in my chair and watched as they passed by the booth in their letter jackets. They were juniors now. I was supposed to be with Pete Thompson, enticing freshmen to join art club, but he'd left school early for his chronic gastrointestinal problems.

You seen my brother, *kitty cat*? Jake called.

I shrugged. Jake's smile slipped away and he and the football players moved on. I immediately spotted Jeffrey standing at the speech team booth, giving a freshman and her parents his best sales pitch.

I turned back in my seat and smoothed out the sketches and paintings on my table. None of them were mine.

They're wonderful paintings, Cat, Mrs. Anderson had said to me as she chose what work would be displayed by her beloved club. But I don't think this is the image we want to put forth.

She didn't like inverted heads, spirals into the abyss, exploding eyes, or the color black.

She did like pastel paintings of El Miller's Welsh corgi, Jiggles.

El Miller had prime real estate at our booth so Jiggles could pant at our visitors. I had a tiny spot in the top corner for a required homework sketch of my dad's car keys. At least my parents weren't coming tonight; Mom, beaming and excited, would ask when I'd be switching all these pictures out for ones of my own, and Dad, having understood immediately what had happened, would hunt Mrs. Anderson down and demand to know why I hadn't gotten more exposure.

I rubbed my face to drag some of the heat from it and ran my fingers back through my hair. My parents weren't here, and they weren't going to be here. All I had to do was smile at the freshmen who came by and try to get them to join.

A booth sign came crashing down at the end of my row. Gamers' club. Ryan Lancaster climbed out from underneath it in a homemade costume. He was a minstrel or a squire or something from a fantasy story, but all his clothes were too big for him, like usual, so he just looked like a theater department reject. He was yelling about unfairness, and assholes, his voice too loud because he hadn't yet learned that no one listened to him. The teachers who ran over to help hurriedly tried to quiet him. A few of Ken Kapoor's henchmen, looking pleased with themselves, stood suspiciously close by.

Jake and the football players, still AWOL from their own booth, laughed at Ryan as they made their way back around. I sank in my chair and smoothed my bangs.

This time Jake didn't glance at me as he passed. They stopped a few booths down, at American Sign Language, and circled up like a pack of hyenas. At the same time, a boy and his parents bounced up to the art club booth looking eager. While I showed the boy our club flyer, I kept the football players in my peripheral vision. They moved strangely, scanning the area like hunters searching for a meal. Jake was no exception to this, but he was the only one who didn't look my direction.

I pointed to Jiggles the Welsh corgi. The boy and his parents found it delightful.

Matt from the football team appeared on the other side of the table.

Cat, he said.

It was always strange to hear a near-stranger say my name as if we were friends.

Are you interested in joining art club? I asked.

No, he said. His raised eyebrow did all the scoffing for him.

Okay, I said.

I have to ask you a question.

I waited.

If Jake Blumenthal asked you out right here, right now, would you say yes?

My body temperature plummeted.

W-what?

You like him, right? Would you go out with him?

The boy enthralled with Jiggles looked between us, not even bothering to be subtle. His parents shifted behind him, keeping their eyes respectfully averted.

Was this supposed to be a real question?

I glanced over at the ASL booth. How could it be a real question when Jake looked so uncomfortable and the others were stifling their laughter with their hands and jackets?

It had to be a trap.

But what if it was real? What if all Jake's teasing was because he liked me? What if I had known all along who he was—someone who could be kind, who could be gentle?

What if it wasn't real?

And, more importantly:

How did they find out that I liked him?

Lightning struck.

I bolted from the booth, leaving Matt and the freshman boy and his parents behind. Matt laughed.

Jeffrey saw me coming, and his face went pale. I dragged him out to the hallway drinking fountains.

Cat! He untangled my fist from his sweater vest. What's wrong?

Matt—Matt on the football team—whatever his name is—asked if I would go out with Jake.

O-okay, what's wrong with that? Isn't that a good thing?

He wiped his hands on his khakis.

No, it's not a good thing! Has Jake ever had trouble talking to a girl he likes? Does he usually get his friends to ask girls out for him?

Well . . . no . . .

I hovered, unable to move, between Jeffrey and the door to the gym. If I avoided the situation, it would surely only get worse. If I went back in, I would have to face Jake and his friends. If only I could tell him that it was okay that he didn't like me back, that I'd expected rejection from the beginning, maybe things would go back to normal. Maybe his friends wouldn't joke about it.

Cat, what is it? Jeffrey asked. He reached for my arm.

What *is* it? I jerked away from him. Why would they ask me that unless they already knew I liked Jake?

His posture shifted. Cat.

Did you tell them?

Cat.

You're the only one who knew, I said.

He scrubbed a hand through his hair. Looked back into the gym, then at his shoes.

It's not like you were great at hiding it, he said. Jake basically figured it out himself.

You could have denied it! I blinked back tears and fisted my hands in the hem of my shirt. If they'd heard it from Jeffrey, they knew it was true. Jake knew it was true.

What's the point? Jeffrey shot back. And why does it even matter? If you ignore them, they'll stop bugging you about it.

They're not *bugging* me; they're *making fun* of me! They

think it's funny that I like your brother, just like I thought they would. That's why I didn't want you to tell anyone! That's why I didn't want anyone to know!

Jeffrey blinked.

Why would you think they'd make fun of you for that? he asked.

Because I'm *weird*! I yelled at him. Heads turned in the gym. Jeffrey opened his mouth to protest, but I spoke over him. I'm that weird girl who does all the creepy drawings and has a lazy eye and wears black turtlenecks all the time! I'm not *allowed* to like boys like Jake!

My chest was filled with poison thorns and broken glass. I couldn't go back into the gym. An invisible barrier physically kept me from going back. Jeffrey didn't get it. He was a boy, and besides that, everyone liked him. Even when they made fun of him, they liked him.

That's completely stupid! Jeffrey grabbed my arm and forced me to face him. *Not allowed?* That's stupid. You're not making any sense.

It's not stupid, I said.

It hurt even more that he was arguing with me.

I have to go, I said.

He released my arm.

I texted Mrs. Anderson to say I was sick, then called my dad to pick me up. He did, without question.

Later that night, I had seven messages and two voice mails from Jeffrey. I ignored them. And there was no way I was going online. I curled up under my covers and tried to wrap my head around going to school tomorrow. I could only run away once.

STARING

I creep closer to investigate the body. The scene is remarkably similar to the scene in the courtyard. The strewn limbs, ripped from their sockets and flung against the wall, the shredded fur, like something took bites out of him. The face smashed in over one cheekbone, the eye socket so misshapen that the eye popped out and rolled away. The only difference is that Mark's blood didn't pool prettily like Julie's; it paints the walls and fans around his body like it was splashed from a can.

There is violence in the air, a thick and oppressive feeling. It's becoming familiar. I don't like that it's becoming familiar.

I turn and run. My heartbeat pounds in my head, filling the echoing silence of the hallways. The halls are the same as they were before. Sometimes School changes things. Sometimes the passage between hallways is at one end, sometimes at the other. Sometimes two hallways are in the same place and you have to walk in and out of a classroom a couple of times to get to the right one. Sometimes the courtyard doesn't exist at all. It's here now, and nothing about it has changed, except that Julie's body is gone. The only sign that she was here is her blood, turned rusty on the stones.

Jeffrey isn't here, either. This is wrong. If things were normal, if he was thinking normally, he would be here trying to understand what was going on. I would tell him that I'd found Mark dead. I would tell him that whoever killed Julie is still out there, still coming after us. And then I wouldn't let him out of my sight again.

I slip out of the courtyard and hurry back to the Fountain Room. More of us are gathered now, huddled like frightened mice. I can't get a good head count, maybe thirty-five; people keep seeming to shift. When I jog in, both fountains spray graceful arcs of brilliant purple water up into the air, as if School is welcoming me back. Sissy emerges from her tent.

"Cat!" she yells, sounding relieved. "Did you hear the noises?"

"What noises?" I ask.

"The screaming, and the . . . something tearing. It was horrible."

"It was Mark," I say, instantly regretting the pallor in Sissy's face. "He's dead. Same as Julie."

Screaming, though? Mark didn't scream. Mark didn't make any noise, ever, because he couldn't speak anymore. Could he?

"So there really is someone out there killing us off," says Pete, his headlight eyes shuttering open and closed.

"What are we supposed to do?" asks El.

"We should stick together!"

"We should go find the asshole and kill *him*."

"It's probably someone from administration."

"What if it's not?"

"Who else could it be?"

"It could be Time and the Hands!"

"Time doesn't care about us. Or them. Or anyone."

"Hey!" My shout quiets the crowd. I can't open my mouth, but the volume of my voice seems limitless. "We don't know who's doing this, or why. We don't know what administration is planning, though it doesn't look like they'll be coming after us anytime soon." I think of Jake's hand pinned to the door and shiver. "We have to work together if we want to catch the person doing this. If you see any suspicious activity, report it to me, okay?"

"Why you?"

"Yeah, what are you gonna do about it?"

What am I going to do about it? *What is anyone else going to do about it?* I want to yell at them. They have been looking to me for answers this whole time, and now when I'm only trying to organize, they act as if I'm stepping out of line. I scan their faces. They fall silent. I *want* them to be scared of my eyes. I want them to know that I am trying to fix something because I feel, somewhere inside me, that another change is coming my way, one that won't be as innocuous as my eyes. "First," I say, keeping my voice calm, "we need to find out who did this. It could be anyone. One of them. One of us. So I'm going to interview everyone as a precaution." There are a few mutters of protest. "Is anyone else here going out in the hallways looking?" I snap at them. "Is anyone else going to risk themselves?"

They are not. They will not.

West asks, "And when you find who's doing this?"

"When I find who's doing this," I say, "I'm going to make sure they never hurt any of us again." I look around the Fountain Room, eager to end the conversation. "Has anyone seen Jeffrey?"

Heads shake. A few muttered no's. I need to find him, but I also need to gather information. The sooner I can cross all of us off the list, the sooner I can find the wretch who did this. But if Jeffrey's out there wandering the halls on his own, even if he's already lost, he's no more protected than Mark.

I ask everyone to line up around the base of the north fountain, and I sit against the base of the south fountain. Sissy helps keep them in line, but they can't stop moving and talking, can't stop staring at the doors. They group with their old friends; the writing club, the radio kids, the artists, the golfers, the theater tech crew. When they come to me, they can hardly stop squirming long enough to answer my questions.

Where were you yesterday around the time of Julie's murder?

Who were you with?

How did you find out about the incident?

Did you see anyone leaving the scene?

Do you have any other information I should know?

I think most of them are too scared to lie. Their answers are all similar.

The Fountain Room.

Everyone else.

Julie's scream.

Just you and Jeffrey.

I didn't do it.

I try to find conflicting information, anything that feels out of the ordinary, but there is nothing. I know that this entire exercise is futile. I'm the star in a clichéd cop drama, already digging the bottom of the barrel for leads. But I have to try.

Sissy is last.

"It's awful here," she says. "Waiting. We all know something is going to happen."

"You're safer together," I say.

"Not when some of us have rusted joints and skin that screams if we move too fast." She glances away. "Or tentacles for arms. Some of us aren't made for fighting back, and that makes us all weaker."

She's never talked like this before. Moans begin to rise behind her, where the others are hiding, hugging each other, or crying.

"Do you think the students from administration did it?" Sissy asks.

"I don't know," I say.

"Then do you have any idea who might have?"

"No."

Her eyes are bright and hard. "Could it be Laserbeams?"

Of course it could. We all know it could be Laserbeams. He is a ghost in the back of our minds. Have any of us ever seen him, or do we just know that he's there, like we know there's someone following us down the dark stairwell at night?

"You didn't want to talk about him before," Sissy says. "But he's a possibility."

"Laserbeams hasn't bothered anyone in a long time," I say. "If he's even still here, we have no reason to believe he did this." But yes, of course it could be him. I know he kills, though I don't know why I know that. Killing is so obviously something he would do that it is *too* obvious. It's too easy. It can't be him.

"He's still here," Sissy says. Her voice is firm and cold, not angry or upset but steely with certainty. With fear that has crystallized into unflinching knowledge that there is something out there worse than Jake and the administration crew, worse than Mark and the other wanderers. I feel it, too, in the pit of my stomach, though I don't remember if Laserbeams was around before, or his identity. What I know is that I don't want to meet him in the dark.

"We shouldn't alarm the others if we don't have to," I say.

"They're already alarmed," Sissy snaps. "They've been thinking about Laserbeams the whole time. Maybe you aren't scared of him, but we are."

She stands and returns to the others before I can reply.

I stand and say, "Thank you all for cooperating. I think it would be best if everyone stayed here for now." There's no reason for anyone to leave, beyond not wanting to stay cooped up.

"Where are you going?" West yells.

"To find Jeffrey," I say. The words are a knife to my stomach. It's been too long already. But Jeffrey's smart; even with what happened with Jake yesterday, he knows how to keep himself safe. He's the only person who knows School's hallways better than I do. I just hope he wasn't too loud or too unaware. "I'm going to find him."

The others stare at me, again, always staring.

They think he's already dead.

.18. ...

Sophomore year.

Still sophomore year.

Images jump and stutter.

The week after the activity fair felt endless. In part because after I got my food the next day, I went to sit at a table by the windows. Alone. There is nothing that makes time go slower than being alone and in pain.

I watched the cafeteria fill, and when Jeffrey got there and came out with his food, I watched him jerk to a halt when he saw our empty table. Watched him look around. He found me, stepped toward me. I dropped my gaze. When I raised it again, he was sitting down at our usual spot. Alone.

I didn't want to argue with him. I didn't want people to

see us together and immediately think of his brother. When I was by myself, I could deal with Raph Johnson passing me in the halls and yelling, *Hey, kitty cat,* Jake says thanks for last night. Making people think I had done things with Jake that I hadn't, that I had done *anything* I hadn't. When I was alone, I sank to the bottom of the river like a stone and I stayed there, hidden.

Week after week after week. After the first month, Mom asked why she hadn't seen Jeffrey around, and I realized how long it had been. I saw Jeffrey as much as I saw anyone; in the hallways, across the cafeteria at lunch, we glanced at each other and went our separate ways. I knew that if I said something, if I responded to one of Jeffrey's texts, everything would be okay again. But when I picked up my phone, I couldn't make my thumbs work. Two letters would have sufficed. One word.

Hi.

Couldn't do it.

At the beginning of November, I looked up from my lunch and saw another girl sitting with Jeffrey at our table. Big teeth, bright clothes. Lane Castillo. They were laughing.

Since when has Lane Castillo hung out with Jeffrey? I asked Sissy during chemistry in sixth period.

Sissy shrugged. I heard Shondra and Lane talking about him during study hall, she said. I think him and Lane are going out.

My brain had to catch up to her words. As Jake's friends, Shondra and Lane had premium access to Jeffrey whenever they wanted it. They'd never wanted it before. Why now?

Jeffrey and Lane? I said. But she's a junior.

So? Sissy said. There are seniors that go out with freshmen.

But it's Jeffrey, I wanted to argue. *Jeffrey doesn't go out with people. Jeffrey doesn't have people.*

Jeffrey has me.

HOMEROOM

I sweep School from top to bottom searching for Jeffrey. Every hallway, every classroom.

I sprint as fast as I can, not pausing to listen to School's strange noises or watch the slow transformation of the building. None of the wanderers could catch me, anyway.

I turn corners and expect to see Jeffrey sprawled on the floor, legs torn from his hips, cardboard head stomped flat. My panic stays in my chest. Nothing is true until I have evidence of it. Until I see Jeffrey's lifeless body with my own eyes, he's not dead.

I only slow down when I get to the hall where I found Mark.

His body is gone. All of him. Cheese and pizza sauce streak the floor where he was, jagged and irregular. Drag-rest, drag-rest. Unless Mark came miraculously back to life and pulled his ruined body away from this place, someone took him.

If Jeffrey were wandering and needed help, but knew he couldn't call for it, where would he go? If I feel safe in the boiler room, where would he feel safe?

I can only think of one place.

Mrs. Remley's room is huge and dark when I get there, just as it was the last time I was here. Mrs. Remley is still behind her desk, already dusty again, and her sadness is palpable. She must know what's been going on.

Soft scratches come from the corner.

"Jeffrey?" I step inside. A hundred desks block the way to the back of the room, where a shape huddles in the shadows. I creep closer, keeping low.

The scratching gets louder. The shape, which looks vaguely rectangular, whimpers.

I peek past the last desk. The shape has two long khaki legs folded up into triangles and two long arms stretched out between them and a tag protruding from the collar of a sweater vest.

"Jeffrey."

I go to him. He curls in on himself, keeping his face from me. He takes a sharp breath and falls silent.

"Why did you leave the boiler room without me?" I ask. "I was worried to death. You know how dangerous it is. I found Mark. He's dead. And whoever did it dragged him off. The killer is still out there. I interviewed the others in the Fountain Room, and none of them have any idea . . . and I kept thinking you'd be next . . . or that you'd gone back to administration and Jake had locked you up. . . . "

He is silent.

"Jeffrey?"

His head rests against his knee and his shoulders bunch up and his arms draw in and at the end of them—at the end of his arms are his hands, but now they're huge and blocky and made of cardboard. The sleeves of his shirt barely hide the squared-off edges of his arms. His chest is all flat planes. His hard, square fingertips scrape the old tile floor, too big to curl into fists, too clunky to grasp objects. The edges of his fingers have already begun to wrinkle and flatten from this incessant scratching, like nails bitten to the beds. I grab his hands to stop him.

"*Jeffrey*. I need you to look at me. I need you to say something."

"I want to leave," he whispers. "Why can't we go home?"

I'm too happy that he's speaking, that he's still there, to care that his eyes have faded almost completely, or that his mouth is etched into a permanent frown, with thick black lines traced in the spaces between his white teeth. He is a caricature drawn by an unhappy child.

I put his arms around me and press my face into his chest. It doesn't feel like I'm holding a boy; it feels like I'm holding a nightmare. His breath rattles around in the cardboard. In-in-in-out.

"I don't want to be here anymore." His fingers scrape against my back. "I want to go *home*, I want to see my mom, I want to leave. Why won't it let us leave, Cat? Where did the doors go?"

"I don't know," I say. It's the only answer I can give him. I don't know where School's doors went. I don't know why it won't let us leave. Maybe my memories will tell me eventually. But there is a killer loose, and that seems like a much more pressing issue than how or when we might escape this place.

He starts sobbing in earnest. I keep my eyes down. I don't want to know how it changes his face. I remember Jeffrey. Jeffrey was soft steel and sweater vests, honeypillar eyebrows and chrysanthemums. Calm, happy light trapped inside a boy.

This isn't what I remember.

This isn't how it's supposed to be.

I can't escape sophomore year.

Is that important?

Is this when it happens?

Jeffrey and Lane Castillo were going to homecoming together. I knew because they showed up on the homecoming ballot.

I stood at my locker holding the little slip of paper, staring at the names. I hadn't voted and I didn't plan to. It was supposed to have been turned in at the end of seventh period anyway. And now I was supposed to be on my way to the art room to pick up the painting I worked on in class today, but my feet didn't want to move. Jeffrey used to meet me at my locker after classes. Now that he didn't, it was harder to get moving.

Hey, kitty cat.

My skin crawled. I turned to the emptying hallway and came face-to-face with Jake Blumenthal. He wore his letter jacket and had his thumbs tucked under the straps of his backpack. His voice was weirdly soft, and for the first time, *kitty cat* didn't sound like a joke.

My first reaction: *Why are you talking to me?*

My revised reaction:

Hi, Jake, I said.

How's it going? he asked.

Fine, I guess. You?

He shrugged.

So, I said.

He smiled a little. That was the undeniable truth about a cute boy's smile: even when the boy made you feel like undeserving trash, his smile never stopped being objectively beautiful. Even when he no longer attracted you, there was always the knowledge that he would attract *someone*, and there was nothing you could do about it.

Things have been weird lately, he said. You don't come over to the house anymore.

Yeah, I said. I hadn't imagined he'd care.

Jeffers has been all mopey.

Isn't he going out with Lane?

Yeah, sort of.

Sort of?

She came over for a party a couple weeks ago and they just sat around.

Did you come here to talk to me about Jeffrey? I asked. For a fleeting moment I thought it might be true, and the floor lifted slightly beneath my feet. But Jake trying to make life easier for his little brother? Why would he waste his precious time on something so frivolous?

Nah, sorry, he said. I actually came to ask you something. Are you going to homecoming?

I folded my arms over my stomach and flattened my back and backpack against the lockers.

No, I said.

He smiled.

Would you want to? he asked. With me?

With you?

Yeah. It'll be fun.

Even after everything he'd ever said, and everything his friends had done, a beautiful, terrible image sprang into my head: me walking into the gym on the arm of star-athlete, angel-faced Jake Blumenthal; pink-cheeked and nervous, feeling unworthy of and amazed at his mere presence; and in the next moment the image morphed into me being burned at the stake by everyone else at homecoming. Everyone who thought I was unworthy, all the girls he didn't ask, Jeffrey standing with Lane, and finally Jake himself. They built the fire with my paintings. My dress is made of paper.

The image was too specific and concrete for the blink of time in which it existed, and when it vanished, I was left with a hollow, rotting feeling in my chest.

When I looked up at Jake, that rotting feeling was all there was.

No, I said.

He smiled again, head cocked to the side.

What?

No, I repeated. No, thank you.

His eyebrows pressed together.

You don't want to go to homecoming with me?

It was more a statement of disbelief than a question.

I shrugged.

Why not? he asked, smiling. Joking. Give me one good reason you won't go with me.

I don't know. I just don't want to.

But why? If you don't have a good reason, then you can't say no.

I was too busy monitoring how close he was getting to point out how nonsensical he sounded. Whatever cologne or body spray he'd waded through that morning clouded the air.

I don't want to, I said. I have . . . something else going on that night.

Like what?

Like . . . I don't remember. I'd have to ask.

So ask. .

I folded my arms close to my body and ducked my head to keep any part of me from touching any part of him.

His arm shot out, hand against the lockers, to stop me from leaving.

Look, he said, I know you like me. I know I've been kind of ignoring you, but I was nervous and I didn't know what to do, so I'm sorry. What's the problem? Is it Jeffrey? 'Cause I can talk to him.

It's not Jeffrey, I said. *It's your face. I used to like it and now I don't and it's too close to me.*

Jake rolled his eyes. Then explain it to me!

I ducked under his arm. He grabbed my shoulder and spun me around so hard my backpack whipped down to my wrist.

I thought you liked me, he said. Were you leading me on? Was this some kind of game?

I stared at him, words forming in my throat like bubbles but popping before I got them out. A game? He was accusing *me* of playing a game with *him*? The absurdity of it wiped all other thoughts from my head.

Sorry, I said. I can't go with you.

I jerked my shoulder from his grasp and hurried to the

end of the hallway, hairs prickling on my neck. I didn't look back.

Around the corner, three of Jake's football friends stood around a locker, apparently engrossed in something they held between them. But when I passed, speed-walking to the art room with my head down and the homecoming ballot crushed in my fist, the three of them started chuckling, and laughed outright when I turned down the next hallway.

Had it been two years before, I would've accepted Jake's offer as soon as the words were out of his beautiful mouth. Even last year I would have. But now my image of him had shifted slightly to the side, and while I could still see his glossy facade, dimpled smile and all, now I could also see the rough, cracking essence underneath.

I got my painting and went home and tried not to think about Jake asking me to homecoming. I managed fine until the next day, in chemistry, when Sissy said, Did Jake talk to you yesterday?

Yeah, I said. Why?

Did he ask you to homecoming?

Yeah.

What did you say?

I said no.

Oh.

Why?

She pulled her beanie down over her ears and looked around like Jake himself might be there.

I heard Shondra and Lane talking in study hall, she said. I guess Jake bet some of his friends that you'd definitely go to homecoming with him, if he asked you. But then you said no, and the football guys have been making fun of him, and he's not very happy about it.

They *bet* on it? I scoffed. Is this a bad movie?

Shondra and Lane kept talking about, like, what a frigid bitch you are, and how you must be a lesbian if you said no to Jake, and—

Thanks, Sissy. I get it.

Sorry, Sissy said. Just, you know, they're not super happy with you right now, so you might want to lay low.

But I was already about as low as I could get.

FLIMSY

Jeffrey can't stand on his own. A light bump knocks him over. He moves like his limbs are filled with sand. I pull his arm over my shoulders and hold his cardboard chest; I prop him up, like a stack of empty boxes.

"Sorry, Cat," he says.

"For what?" I say.

His left leg buckles. I stop him from falling to the floor.

"This," he says.

I hold his hand to keep his arm over my shoulders. It's twice as big as it used to be, cartoonishly big, and his fingers dwarf mine. I want to ask if he can still feel. He probably can. I can't take my gloves off, and I can still feel, so why couldn't he?

We hobble to the Fountain Room. The boiler room is probably

safer, but I don't want him to be alone. And I'm a little worried he might catch on fire. Someone needs to stay with him. It can't be me.

I take Jeffrey to Sissy, who wraps him up in blankets and hides him away in the corner of her tent, where he'll be safe until he's ready to come out and speak to the others. Some of them are already drifting over, curious.

"I'll be back," I tell Sissy.

"Where are you going?" Jeffrey crawls from the tent on hands and knees.

I'm very aware of my face not moving, of my eyes not blinking, when I turn to him and say, "I'm going to talk to Time."

.20. . . .

Bitch.

Lesbian.

They didn't faze me.

I could definitely be a bitch, and people who used their homophobia for insults were assholes. Even getting ignored by anyone who liked Jake didn't hurt, because I didn't care about most of those people.

A week after I turned Jake down, I went to open my locker and got a handful of snot and spit instead. I whipped my hand away. A webbing of goo spanned the spaces between my fingers. I ran to the bathroom for paper towels.

Whatever. It wasn't like a loogie could hurt me.

Two days later, I was working on a sketch at lunch. The

cafeteria as a wide turbulent river, the tables as wreckage being torn apart by the rapids, students as survivors struggling to stay above the surface. Some of them were half underwater, changing into sea creatures; some of them were standing atop the tables and trying to shove the others beneath the water. The paper was swiped from under my pencil. Raph Johnson stood in front of me, holding it up so the small group of kids clustered behind him could see.

Interesting, he said. In this, I see a very disturbed mind. What do we think, class?

A chorus of agreement sounded from the others.

I concur, he said.

He ripped the picture in half, then in fourths, then in eighths, then slid it back underneath my pencil.

Destroying your pictures isn't good, *kitty cat*, he said. You're never going to accomplish anything like that.

He and his sidekicks walked off, laughing.

I set my pencil down on the table before I snapped it in half. I knew it was a good picture, even if it was just a sketch. I knew Raph wouldn't know good art if it punched him in the balls. I knew even if he *did* know good art, he would've said the picture was bad and ripped it up anyway, because whether it was good or not wasn't the point; the point was that I had drawn it.

I piled the pieces on my lunch tray with the other trash

and got up to dump it. The garbage and recycling cans were next to Jeffrey's table—my old table—and now that he was there every day with Lane, it was awkward. I tried to dump my trash without seeing them, but then I turned and there they were, making out. Lane looked like she was trying to eat his face. Jeffrey looked puzzled. He leaned away from her. She climbed on top of him.

I turned away, my blood pressure threatening to blow the top of my head off and cover Pompeii in ash. It wasn't that she was kissing Jeffrey, because Jeffrey could kiss anyone he wanted. It was that she'd somehow convinced him to waste his time on *her*, when he should have been wasting it on *me*. That was *my* seat at *my* table and *my* best friend she was groping in public.

I joined the crowd funneling out of the cafeteria and stopped in the alcove by the restrooms to catch my breath.

A finger brushed against my shoulder. I flattened myself into the corner.

It was only Jeffrey.

Hey, he said. His honeypillar eyebrows pressed together in a frown.

Hi, I said. I *could* say it now. It was like fresh air after a long time shut inside.

Can we talk? he asked. After school, maybe?

Sure, I said. Where?

Why not here?

Sounds good.

Cool.

He started to walk away. Rubbed his neck. Turned back.

Are you okay? he asked.

Are *you* okay? I replied.

He smiled a little.

See you, he said.

I made it through the rest of the day without too much trouble, except I got shoved in the back once, and in chemistry Sissy asked me not to sit quite so close to her so people didn't start calling us the lesbian couple. El Miller, who sat across from us and had just said good-bye to her girlfriend in the hallway, gave Sissy the most scathing look I'd ever seen and picked up her things to move to the other side of the lab.

Jeffrey was waiting for me by the restrooms outside the cafeteria after seventh period. He leaned against the wall, checking his phone, his other hand tucked into his pocket. He looked like the perfect little cutout of the studious boy, kempt and orderly and ready to do homework. He and Jake were a complementary pair: perfect student, perfect athlete.

Hey, I said.

Jeffrey shoved his phone in his pocket. Hey.

Texting Lane? I asked.

He shook his head. She doesn't like to text. Besides, we—ah—broke up.

You broke up? When? You didn't seem very broken up at lunch.

You mean the weird making out thing? That was right after I told her we should break up.

You told her you wanted to break up, so she made out with you?

Jeffrey shrugged.

Why did you break up with her?

We didn't have anything in common.

Didn't you hang out with her outside of school?

Yeah, a bit.

What did you talk about?

We . . . didn't talk.

Oh.

He shrugged again and said, It wasn't anything extreme. She wanted to kiss for, like, five-minute intervals, and then she'd say something about being a good Christian, and then we'd kiss again.

Well, congrats, I said. You've officially hit *Made Out in School* status. I don't think I'll hit that milestone unless it's with another girl, which most of the school seems to think is likely. I'm actually not against it, but at this point it would feel like putting on a show for a bunch of assholes. . . .

What happened? he asked. What did Jake do?

I'm surprised you didn't hear about it.

I did, but from people who weren't there. And from Jake.

What did Jake say?

Just stuff I don't want to repeat. I've never heard him be that mad for that long before. I think you embarrassed him.

Good.

So what did he do?

Cornered me by my locker and asked me to homecoming. He made a nineties movie bet with his friends that I'd say yes. Because, you know, I'm that desperate. I said no, and he kept asking why and saying if I didn't give him a good reason, then I had to say yes.

Jeffrey said, He let you leave, right?

Yeah, after he almost ripped my arm out of its socket trying to keep me there.

Jeffrey rubbed his eyes. I'd punch him for you if I didn't think he'd break my neck.

I'd punch him myself if I didn't think people would start calling me a crazy wild redneck monster bitch instead of just a bitch.

I'm sorry I told him you liked him. This wouldn't have happened.

It's not your fault.

He was quiet for a moment—that quintessential Jeffreytype quiet, where he wanted to keep arguing until I folded and let him take the blame—but he finally let it go and sighed.

So, he said, are you going to come back to the table, or should I move to the windows? Tomorrow is pizza stick day. It'd be a shame to miss it.

It was always a shame to miss pizza stick day.

TIME

The hallways are shrinking. The lockers are a few inches shorter, the floor tiles centimeters smaller, the ceiling now visible. I have a longer line of sight, and it unsettles me more than the darkness. Now I can see what's coming for me.

The first thing we did was search for a way out. There are still doors and windows, but only inside, leading to classrooms or restrooms or some other mutated space. There are no doors or windows to the outside. School has taken them away from us, and no matter how often we ask for them back, no matter how many sacrifices we make, none of them have been returned. The only view to the outside—or what we assume is the outside— is the blinding white sky above the courtyard. After a while we gave up looking for more. Jake and the others retreated to administration, and we took over the Fountain Room.

There is only one person who might know something the rest of us don't. Only one person who spends his days collecting information, who is neither Us nor Them, who would both thrive in this nightmare and desperately want out of it.

His name is Time, and he lives in the auditorium.

I think School and Time have come to some sort of agreement. Everything within thirty feet of the auditorium is coated in gold—the floors, the walls, the light fixtures—like a tomb for an ancient conquering king. I creep past the main hallway, past administration, past the gym—where Mr. Gabel, the gym teacher, drips off the bleachers and disappears through the floor—and into the arts wing, where empty instrument cases still sit on their racks, unfinished paintings lean against doorframes, and papers litter the floor. If the rest of the school looks abandoned, the arts hallways look like a flood came through and left wreckage. This is Time's territory.

I turn down the hallway to the auditorium. Rich sapphire drapes cover the walls and ceiling and lead the way to a massive golden entrance watched over by the god Vishnu and a thousand snakes carved from ivory and gold. Two large columns flank the doorway to the theater. Golden cobras wrap around the columns, ruby eyes winking, hoods flared at anyone who approaches. I've never been close enough to them to see the detail in their design; the edges of their scales are words etched in a calligraphic script I can't read.

I push my way through a curtain of beads on long strings. I suppose it's a testament to Time's comfort here that he doesn't have anyone guard his doors. Massive plants burst right out of the floor, creating a second, shorter hallway. As I pass, their leaves change color from blue to purple to black. I wade through and past two date palms that have another curtain strung between them. Behind that is the auditorium.

I've been to a lot of events here, and it looks nothing like it used to. The two aisles sweep out to the sides and stretch to the stage. The chairs have been removed and replaced with a single massive porthole that looks down into water; a huge, dark shape occasionally glides past. The tank of water itself must extend far beneath the auditorium to hold a creature that size. Perhaps it's not a tank at all. Perhaps School sits on water. Perhaps the ocean is beneath us, and we never knew.

On the sides of the stage are two computer terminals that look right out of an eighties sci-fi movie, each manned by two of Time's Hands. In the center of the stage sits Time himself on a tall throne spun from gold, made from the shapes of Tetris pieces. He sits sideways, his back against one arm and his legs thrown over the other, a clock balanced against his chest and an old Game Boy in his hands. Flanking his throne are two ten-foot-tall stuffed Saint Bernards, like toys for a giant toddler.

I make sure Time sees me well before I reach him. He is the last person I want to take by surprise.

The Hands don't look up from their work. The creature glides past the porthole and a shudder runs through me, knowing that it's beneath my feet. Time swears loudly and smashes his fingers against the buttons of his Game Boy. I climb the steps and stand in the stage lights.

"Time," I say.

Finally, he looks up.

We all wanted him, once. I suppose we all still want him. We want what he has.

He smiles behind his Wayfarers.

"I love what you've done with your eyes, Cat Lady."

.21......

No one at school knew where I lived.

Only Jeffrey.

My house was an island in a sea of mist, quiet and overgrown with flowers and small trees. Everyone knew my mom's nursery, the Little Leaf, but not many people realized there was a house attached to it. I liked the anonymity. It kept me safe through sophomore year, when anyone who had any remote connection to Jake began thinking I was the scum of the earth and scrawled my name and other things on restroom stalls.

So that spring, when Mrs. Anderson assigned a realistic painting of our homes as our class final, my stomach sank. Not only was realism something I didn't normally go for, but the paintings would be displayed in the cases in the main hallway, as the art finals always were. As soon as anyone saw the nursery, they'd make the connection that it wasn't just a store, but my house.

I can't do the final, I said to Mrs. Anderson after the bell rang that day.

I know it's not the doom and gloom you like, she said, waving a hand, but you'll do wonderfully, Cat. If you work really hard on this one, we could enter it for the state arts award. And I'm not kidding, you could win. I don't think they'll accept any of your . . . your usual work, but a lovely, realistic edifice done in oil . . . they'll love that.

I stood there with the assignment paper held tentatively between my fingers.

It's such a big scholarship, Cat. If you wanted to keep doing art, you could go somewhere like New York, really get into it. Your style is certainly unique, but if you can show them you have range—

It's not the style, I said. Realism is fine. I just . . . don't want to do my house.

I looked over my shoulder. I don't want people to know where I live.

Oh, she said. Well, you wouldn't have to put the address on it.

They'd recognize it.

She frowned. I suppose if it really matters that much to you, you could do a painting of something *around* your house. Something specific to you, that captures the essence of your home rather than the house itself. How does that sound?

My insides uncurled.

I can do that.

Do you have anything in mind?

No. Not right now.

Why don't you come back tomorrow with something, and we'll talk about it.

When I went home that night, there was nothing to see but bonsai trees. In the shop, but also all over the house, under heat lamps and on strict watering regimens, most of them basking in the sun on the back porch. I had watched many of them grow as I grew: jade trees with their green coin leaves; jacaranda dripping with azure blooms; prickly juniper; a little nub of a crabapple, bearing fruit; a pine tree pruned into beautiful domed tiers. There was going to be a bonsai tree somewhere in my damn painting, that was for sure. The only question was which one.

Dad was no help. He didn't get why I couldn't take a photo of the storefront and paint it. He said it would be good advertising, because I guess teenagers are all about buying herb kits. Mom said that any of the trees would work equally well, because she'd made them all, just like she'd made me, and they were all beautiful, like me. Her words, not mine. I ended up on the chair on our cramped back porch, hidden among a tiny forest, with my phone camera open in my lap and daylight fading around me.

A few minutes passed before Mom wheeled her favorite juniper on a cart out to the center of the deck where she would prune it. It was old and massive for a bonsai, its bleached trunk curling around itself, spiraling over its own branches and prickly foliage like a white wave. From my vantage point in the trees, Mom looked like a giant towering over a forest, sculpting the Earth. The sun glowed orange behind her, outlining her shape. Her hands moved gracefully among the branches.

I took several pictures of her without saying anything. If she knew what I was doing, she'd make some silly face or go stiff and lose her surreal nature. The pictures were clear and crisp, the colors perfect.

I didn't often get excited about painting still life or portraiture, but this was different. I could already imagine it spilling out onto a canvas, the layers of paint, the blending of the colors, exactly how my hand would move as I made the lines of the juniper.

Mom, I said. I'm doing a painting of you for my final.

A painting of me? she said, without looking up. A painting of me doing what?

This.

That'll be a little boring, don't you think? Should I make a face to liven it up?

Too late. I already have the pictures.

She smiled and said, You'll have to show me when it's done.

LOUD
NOODLE

"**W**hy are you carrying around Mrs. Flowers?" I point to the wall clock cradled in Time's arms.

"She's a cool teacher," he replies. "Thought she'd be bored alone. Speaking of alone, where's your better half?"

"Indisposed," I say, glancing around at Time's four Hands. They hadn't turned to look at us, though I know they must be listening.

Time straightens in his throne. "Don't tell me he had a run-in with the creepy creep slinking around here slashing throats. That's what you came here to ask me about, isn't it?"

"How did you know about that?"

"About Julie the Tear Factory getting slaughtered in the courtyard? How would I *not* hear about that?" He motions to the computers. "Listen, Catmandu, not a thing goes on in this school that I don't know about. I know you went to administration and accused the big man of killing Wisnowski, and he cut his hand off and nailed it up as a declaration of war. Now you're afraid he might send out the goon squad to hurt the rest of you, am I right?"

"Well," I say, "you're not wrong."

"Don't worry. Blumenthal's not leaving administration, and neither are any of his friends. They're more scared than you are."

"What about you?" I say. "Have you been out there? Do you know what it is?"

"Does it look like I ever leave this place?" He balances Mrs. Flowers on his chest and throws his arms out wide. His many treasures gleam from the dark edges of the stage. "Why would I? The Hands find something and they bring it back. No one gets brutally slaughtered; nothing changes. There's a reason I didn't get involved in the stupid feud between you and your administration friends. If any of those bastards try to come in here, we feed them to Ajax."

"Who's Ajax?"

Time nods at the porthole in the floor.

"You feed them to your sea monster?"

"Who else am I going to feed them to? They give Macaroni and Forte tummy aches." He reaches out to stroke one of the two big stuffed dogs, whose glassy eyes stare blankly into the distance. "By the way, you should be glad they're so well trained. They love chasing cats."

"You never answered my question," I say. "Do you know what's out there? It didn't just kill Julie. It got Mark, too."

"Chubby Mark? That guy was still around?"

Clearly Time does *not* know everything. If I had teeth, they'd be grinding. "What's doing this? What's killing us?"

"Hey, Time?" One of the Hands looked back over his shoulder, his fingers frozen on the keyboard. Time's expression morphs into annoyance. He raises an eyebrow. "S-sorry," the Hand stutters. "I just—I have a question."

"What?" Time snaps.

"Is 'Punjabi' capitalized?"

Time's cherry red Converse slam to the floorboards. He leans forward in his seat, teeth gleaming, and yells, "Do you capitalize 'English'? What about 'Spanish' or 'French'? Do you?"

"Do I—yes."

"Yeah, you do! Put the pieces together, Tod, you racist fuck! If you can't get something that simple right, I'll get someone else to write the memoir!"

"Got it, sorry. I'll do it right. Promise."

"Good." Time relaxes and turns back to me, swiping his dark hair off his forehead. "What were we talking about again, Cat Lady?"

There was a time when I wanted the safety Time could

provide, but I'm glad now that I never took it.

"I'm going to make this quick," I say. "I know you don't like giving out information for free, so I'm going to tell you what I want to know, and you're going to tell me what it's going to cost."

He taps a foot on the floor in time with the ticking of Mrs. Flowers's second hand. His Wayfarers hide his eyes, though I can feel his gaze on me. I hope he can feel mine, too. Finally, he smiles.

"Do you know *why* Blumenthal is more scared than you?" Time asks. "I'll tell you. It's because you understand this nightmare we're all in. Maybe you don't know why we're all here, but you know what that thing is out there, killing people. You know where it comes from."

"I don't. I just asked you because I *don't* know—"

He swipes a hand through the air, swatting my comment away. "You *know*, even though you think you don't, and Blumenthal has *no goddamn clue*, even though it's hunting him, too." He smiles again, bigger, whiter. "And he won't know until it jumps out of the shadows and strangles him."

.22. ....

Spring.

Sophomore year.

The endless stretch.

Oil painting was annoying. It took forever to finish. It couldn't be in sunlight. You had to deal with fumes. You needed a huge work area. You had to have a place to store the painting and supplies when you weren't using them, because oil paints didn't dry for days and you had to mix big batches of color and you had to varnish it when it was all done. And worst of all, the supplies were expensive. Cheap supplies usually come back to bite you in the ass, which is one of the great truths of art. They don't mix or spread right; they don't last.

Not all art is meant to last. Some art is beautiful for how fleeting it is. Some is meant to be destroyed, and that's what makes it art. I wanted this to be around forever.

The task of creating the oil painting took my mind off everything else. I was sure Jake and his friends were keeping up their onslaught, but I stopped paying attention. I worked on my painting in art class and after school every day, shoving my other homework to the side; the back corner of the art room became my castle, and while I painted, the drawbridge was up. It was just me and my mom and her bonsai, and my brushstrokes bringing them to life. On Fridays Jeffrey usually didn't have anything to do after school, so I let him sit on a stool and watch me with the stipulation that he couldn't talk.

One Friday I looked up at the clock and realized it was nearly five, three hours after school had ended.

Why didn't you stop me? I asked Jeffrey while I scrambled to put away my supplies. Students weren't allowed in the art wing past five o'clock unless there was an event going on.

You were really into it, he said. And you told me I'm not allowed to talk if I want to keep watching.

I huffed as I gathered my brushes. When I straightened, my head bumped Jeffrey's chin; he'd leaned forward to get a better look at the painting.

It looks amazing, Cat, he said, his voice soft. I don't know how you do this.

I just pay attention, I said.

No, he said. It's more than that.

I kept my head down and went to clean my brushes.

FINGERS

I say nothing and wait for Time to answer me.

Eventually, he does.

"Okay, Cat Lady. You want to know who the killer is."

"That's it. What do you want for it?"

"If I tell you, are you going to go find this person and try to stop them?"

"That's the plan."

He shakes the Game Boy at me. "Good woman. It's your lucky day, because it appears our interests are aligned. He has something of mine. Promise me that when you take him out, you'll get my property back, and I'll tell you who it is and where you can find him. It should be easy enough once he's dead."

I don't answer at first. I'm not sure now what I thought I was actually going to do. Reason with the person? In this place? There is more than a real possibility that stopping a killer means killing him myself.

I say carefully, "What is it that he has?"

Time eases back in his chair, as if readying himself for storytime. "I was the first one here," he says. "Don't ask me how I knew I was the first, I just did. Then the Hands showed up, then the rest of you. And the last one to get here—you know who the last one to get here was? I'll give you a hint: his name starts with 'L' and ends with 'ass-backward aserbeams.'"

My heart sinks, though I knew he would say Laserbeams. Of course I knew. This is the one thing we all know: Laserbeams is deadly.

"He sat around in the hallway for a day or two and then he went and made his own kingdom in School's bowels, deeper even than your boiler. Called it *Knifeworld*. He even put a big banner up, like it's the grand opening of a theme park." Time is so animated I think he might chuck his Game Boy at me. "And Knifeworld is really close to my auditorium, you know, so I thought I'd go and welcome the guy and explain how territory works, and that he'd better stay out of mine. And that guy—that great, genial guy—guess what he does?"

"What?"

Time rips a brown-flesh-colored glove off his right hand and shoves his hand at me. His middle, ring, and pinkie fingers are missing. My stomach turns.

"That little fuckface is wearing my digits like jewelry!"

The stumps wiggle like worms chopped in half. Time slips the glove back on, fits the fake fingers back into place. Once on, the glove is indistinguishable from his skin.

"I want my fingers back," he says. "And I want that dick to feel the pain."

"So Laserbeams is the one killing us all," I say, feeling hollow, "and you want me to go get your fingers back."

"That's it, Catsup."

The Hands are looking at us now, their work abandoned. I knew Laserbeams lived in Knifeworld—everyone knows that—and that Knifeworld was not a place I wanted to go, but everything else is new information. We've all wondered who he is, but no one dares go near. There were times I thought knowing more about Laserbeams would make him less terrifying, might reveal part of him that would make him seem like the rest of us. But wearing fingers like jewelry does not make him seem like the rest of us.

This is a suicide mission. I know it, and Time knows it. But what else is there for me? Am I supposed to let more of us get picked off until the only people left are me and Jake and Time? I can't afford to wait for my memories to return, and School isn't offering up any solutions, so I'll have to create some for myself.

"I'll do it," I say, stomach lurching. "Tell me how to get to Knifeworld, and I'll get your fingers back." The entrance to Knifeworld moves, but I'm sure the Hands keep track of it.

Time's grin is huge. "Just what I wanted to hear. You'll love this. Down the hall, take a left and two rights. It's in the boys' restroom today."

"Knifeworld is in the boys' restroom?"

"The entrance is."

"Fine." I stand there, not wanting to leave yet. "Why not you? Why don't you go kill Laserbeams, get your fingers back? You know things about him no one else does. You have your Hands to back you up."

"What good is power if you can't get someone else to do your dirty work?" Time pokes absently at the Game Boy buttons and glances at me over the tops of his Wayfarers. He won't meet my gaze directly.

"You're scared of him," I say.

Time scoffs. "Scared of that loser—"

"You don't understand him, either. And you're scared of him."

He falls silent. His jaw clenches. "Careful, Cat."

"Threats, Time?" I ask. "Sounds like you might be a little scared of me, too."

He says nothing to that. There's nothing left to say. I turn to leave.

"Wait, Cat Lady," Time says. I turn to find him reaching into his back pocket, pulling out a switchblade. He flicks it open.

"It's dangerous to go alone," he holds the blade out to me. "Take this."

.23......

I finished the painting.

When I held it up, completed, for the first time, I felt comfort in knowing that my mother would tend to her bonsai in the sunset forever. On the back of the canvas, in very small letters, I wrote the title of the piece: *Protector.*

When can I see it? Mom asked me that night, as I worked on a sketch instead of studying for my calculus final. She'd asked me at least once a week since I'd told her about it.

You could see it if you were coming to the art fair, I said. But *no*, you and Dad have an exhibit opening to go to....

She huffed at her crossword, jabbing her pen my direction without looking at me. The juniper is the central piece! I wish I could go to your fair, but I'll be able to see it after that, right?

Yeah, you'll be able to see it after that. I'll bring it home before I have to send it to be judged for the scholarship.

Mrs. Anderson was going to help me pack up the painting and ship it. First place was almost a full ride to certain schools. Good ones. I could actually do art somewhere. But there were going to be a lot of people entering.

I darkened the thick curve of a line on my sketch. The face was a cat mask, white and porcelain smooth, but the neck and shoulders were human.

Mom watched me over the top of her paper.

What? I asked.

You're smiling, she said.

So?

Does Mrs. Anderson think you'll do well?

She was the one who told me to enter.

Do *you* think you'll do well?

I hesitated for a moment before I said, Yes.

I didn't know what my competition would be like. I had no idea what far corners of the country they'd send their work from or what sort of things they'd portray and with how much emotion. But I knew my work, and I knew how it made me feel. When I pulled out my canvas and paints in the art room, I knew how easy the colors and the brushstrokes came.

I knew that outpouring of creativity brought relief. My usual dark, surreal drawings sometimes felt like pulling teeth, but the oil painting never had.

I'd produced it with such clarity that I had never questioned what I was doing.

Something like that was too rare to doubt.

KNIFEWORLD

Two lefts and a right get me to the entrance to Knifeworld, aka the boys' bathroom in the middle of what might be the math hallway or what might be the science hallway or what might be half of the math hallway and half of the science hallway stitched together in the middle. The door looks like the door to any bathroom, except the little male figure on the placard has no head. I push it open and peer inside. I'd never been in a boys' restroom before. Urinals line one wall, sinks the other, and a few stalls on the far wall have been ripped out to make way for a portal to hell.

It's a large black hole with a flagstone staircase leading downward. Glass shards gleam in the darkness, and a sound emanates up from its pit—something between wailing wind and pigs being led to slaughter. I creep forward and realize that there *is* wind. A soft breeze, a little moist, blows from the hole. The walls of the tunnel are wet, and they undulate. A throat. The wind is both warm and cool at the same time, and reeks of eggs and spoiled milk.

One stall door, hanging by a hinge, has a small sign made of poster board on it. A thick black arrow points to the hole, and the words above the arrow read "Knifeworld This Way."

I cannot fathom why Time was ever enticed to go down there.

As soon as I set foot on the stairs, a feeling of claustrophobia worms up my spine.

The tunnel might cough and contract on me.

The little pieces of glass in its walls will stick me through like an iron maiden.

I crouch low, making myself as small as possible. Something moist and sticky drips into my hair, onto my mask and shoulders, but when I raise a hand to swipe it away, there is nothing there. In my other hand I clench Time's switchblade.

It doesn't seem useful to bring a knife into a place called Knifeworld, but I feel better for having it. Hopefully, Laserbeams will be soft enough to stab.

No one likes Laserbeams. No one wants Laserbeams here. Not the changed hunkered down in the Fountain Room, not Jake and the others in administration, not even Time. That must make what I'm about to do at least a little okay.

The tunnel twists in and around and back on itself several

times, and before I reach the end, the darkness becomes complete. I make my way down by feeling the flagstone steps beneath my gloves. At the very bottom a bright light snaps on suddenly—a white room. A small, white box of a room that the tunnel leads into. There's an open door on the other side with a large sign posted above it.

KNIFEWORLD

FUN FOR ALL AGES

I hold the switchblade flat against my thigh and creep through the door into a long, dark hallway.

It's like School had a hidden basement we never knew about. The floor is the same as the hallways above, and the ceiling and walls are so far away they're shrouded in darkness, School at its fullest inhale. I keep going. I stare into the darkness ahead and can't see anything, and into the darkness where the walls should be and see less. There is nothing here.

The chime of metal on metal sounds above my head. I glance up and catch a wink of light in the dark. A soft breeze blows from the unseeable edges of the room, and the chime rings again. And again and again, all over the place, above me. Flashflashflash. Gleams in black. Sharp edges.

There are knives hanging from the ceiling.

Huge knives. Aslongasmybody knives. Knives that would have to be held up with massive chains. When there is no wind, the knives don't move, and they become darkness. But now that I know they're up there, I can feel them. Waiting to fall.

I continue on. I make myself as small as possible and ignore the twisting of my gut.

I wish I was back upstairs in the Fountain Room. With Jeffrey, with the others. Safe in Sissy's quilt tent. I imagine I am, and that everything is okay, and it becomes a little easier.

It feels like I've been walking for years when I reach a small, cylindrical pedestal rising from the floor. I can just see it in the dim light. It is carved from stone with intricate details etched into its sides, like it has been stolen from an Aztec temple. The outline of a left hand is carved into its top, fingers spread. Small white dots have been painted in the spaces between the fingers.

Another sign, similar to the one on the restroom stall door, has been taped on the pedestal so anyone who approaches can read it.

five-finger fillet

test your skills

I know this game, but I don't remember why. I'm examining the pedestal from all sides when the wind blows again, and the knives above rattle and flash.

A voice from the dark says, "I see you brought your own blade."

The art show.

Our arts program was decent enough, but we didn't get much funding. Most of the money the school received went into technology or sports, because those things made the money back. But once a year we got some kind of grant to put on an art show at the end of the spring semester, and those rich people who funded the grant came out and looked at our work, and parents and other students were there, and we all had to get dressed up and be nice.

I hadn't presented at the show my freshman year. I hadn't wanted to. My art was weird and I knew it, and I didn't like the looks people gave it when they saw it. They didn't know what to ask or say. They didn't know how to react. Plus Mrs.

Anderson would've stuck me and my art in a nook somewhere anyway, and no one would find me.

This year I wanted to do it. And after I showed Mrs. Anderson the painting, she gave me the prime spot in the middle of the gym where everyone would see me and my painting whether they wanted to or not. Three pieces would be featured in the center on a raised platform, each facing a different direction. Mine faced the gym doors.

When we were done setting up, I pulled my nice clothes out of my locker and went to the girls' restroom to change. My hands sweated as I pulled on my black pants; the button slipped out of my fingers twice. The second time, I laughed. I'd never had so much nervous energy before. So much *good* nervous energy. I had only ever been anxious when I knew someone was going to look at my art. Now that I *knew* my work was good, now that I *knew* I had something, even if it wasn't what I normally made, I wanted people to see it. I wanted to know what they thought. I wanted someone else to feel what I felt when I watched Mom tending her trees. That serenity, the relief that some small piece of the world is in the hands of someone who knows exactly how things should be.

I made it to my post twenty minutes before the doors opened. I stared at my painting, checking it over for any stray hairs or marks. I knew everything was fine; I had checked the painting itself enough times to know that I didn't want to change anything. That I *shouldn't*. Sometimes a piece of art could be altered and made better, and sometimes, even though something can always be fixed, it shouldn't be.

Ready, Cat? Mrs. Anderson passed behind me.

I think so, I said.

Good, she said. They're going to love it.

And they did. When the doors opened and the first visitors came in, I watched their eyes travel to the middle of the room, up the platform, and fix on my painting. Watched them gravitate toward it. They looked at the other displays they passed, parents went to check on their children's work, but each and every person eventually made it to me, and their questions came like a waterfall.

Is this in oils? It's so crisp!

The subject is so beautiful and subtle—who is it?

Did you do this from a picture? Did you take it?

Are you planning to paint for a career when you get older? You've really got something here.

I answered their questions as best I could. Sometimes it was just praise, and I didn't know what to do, so I muttered awkward thank-yous and caught myself averting my eyes the way Mom did whenever someone complimented her trees. Finally, when there was a lull, I tucked my hair behind my ears and rubbed my face, trying to work some of the heat out. The gym was always warm, and the attention made it worse.

Still, it was good. Good nerves. I'd be exhausted when I got home tonight.

I saw Jeffrey bounding toward me long before he reached me. His smile was huge, and after a second I realized it was because *my* smile was huge.

He gathered me up in a hug.

How's it going? he asked, squeezing tight before letting me go. I guess I don't even have to ask, judging by the swarm of admirers that just left.

I laughed. That's all you need to know, I said. It's been . . . intense.

As it should be. This is the best painting here. God, Cat, you're definitely going to win that scholarship. There's no way you can't. It looks amazing.

My cheeks burned hotter than they had all night. I punched him in the arm.

Shut up, I said.

Seriously, though, Cat.

I know, I know.

He grinned. Shoved his hands in his pockets. Glanced away for a second.

What? I asked.

Ah, he said. I should probably tell you that Jake is here.

What alarmed me most was how quickly the smile fell off my face.

Why is he here? I asked. What for?

Well, we only have one car, Jeffrey said. So if I wanted to come, I had to go with him. And Shondra's presenting today, too.

Jeffrey motioned to a table off to my right, where Shondra Huston was showcasing a series of watercolors she'd been working on all year. I'd only seen her art in the cubbies where we kept our current projects. Jake stood with her, a lazy arm looped around her waist, glancing over her pieces. His back was to me, thankfully.

They're going out now, Jeffrey said. For like a month or two.

I hadn't noticed. I'd been too wrapped up in my painting.

Oh, I said. Well.

Yeah.

Does she—is she over at your house a lot?

Yeah, actually, Jeffrey said. Whenever Jake is home. But they mostly stay in his room, so I don't see them much.

A note of sadness tinged his voice, but it was offset by the easy smile that reappeared. Such a lie. Jeffrey didn't lie about the little things, but he was always lying about the way he felt, and he was good at it. He'd had a lot of practice. Pretending it didn't hurt when Jake went out of his way to find anyone else to spend time with. Pretending he didn't want Jake's approval, or his attention.

I studied Jake and Shondra. For too long. Jake turned and they both caught me looking. Jake said something to Shondra. They headed our way.

Oh, no, I said.

Jeffrey moved closer to my side.

We're going to go get something to drink, Jake said to Jeffrey, voice cool. Want anything?

No, thanks, Jeffrey said.

No one's coming to my booth anyway, Shondra said, pulling her hair to one side and fanning her neck. Looks like you've gotten a ton of love, though, Cat.

I didn't miss the jealousy. Last year she'd had my spot on the platform, facing the doors. This year she had done a beautiful seasonal panorama, and it was no secret she had assumed she'd have the whole platform to herself.

Yeah, it's nice, I said, as calmly and as evenly as I could. No tone. No inflection. I gave them a small smile. *Please walk away. Please leave me alone and walk away.*

Is that your mom? Jake took a step toward me.

Yeah, I said. I shrank back against the platform, trying to shield the painting from him, but he just looked up at it with a bored expression and made a little *hm* in his throat and tugged on Shondra's arm.

Let's go, he said.

I let out my breath.

He's trying to psych you out, Jeffrey said, watching Jake and Shondra retreat. He's an athlete; that's what they do. Don't worry about it.

I'm not worried, I said.

I wasn't. I wouldn't allow myself to be. There was nothing they could do to me anymore. Even if I didn't win that scholarship, I had something. I was *good*. Maybe not good enough to sell paintings for millions of dollars, or to have my own gallery show, but I had something they didn't.

They couldn't take who I was from me.

FIVE-FINGER FILLET

"**W**ho's there?" is my least favorite question. It sounds so weak and pitiful. As soon as it's spoken, everyone who hears it knows that someone is frightened. Someone is afraid and in the dark. Someone is looking wildly from side to side, aware that they're being hunted but unable to spot the hunter.

I yell it.

He laughs. High and reedy, like a boy who hit puberty but stalled in that place where his voice always cracks.

"Don't be scared, Cat. We're going to play. It'll be fun."

"How do you know my name?"

"Call it a lucky guess."

Chills creep across my mask, and I remember that my mask doesn't hide my face, because it *is* my face.

"Are you Laserbeams?" I ask.

"Why don't we play first, and if you win, I'll tell you?"

It's him. "No," I say quickly, "if I win, I want Time's fingers."

There's a strange, almost audible pause; though I can't see him, I can sense he's taken aback by this, maybe even holding in a laugh.

"Time's fingers?" he says. "That silly goose. If he wanted his fingers, he could have asked me for them. He knows that."

Definitely Laserbeams.

"Time doesn't seem to think so," I say. "If I win the game, can I have them?"

"I don't see why not, if that's the prize you want. Would you like to hear what will happen if you lose?"

"Sure."

"Here's what will happen if you lose: I will close the door and you will stay here forever with me and my friends."

What kind of friends could Laserbeams have, here in this empty place? Unless this was some cute way of him saying he was going to kill me. That seemed much more likely.

Suicide mission. I knew this. I came anyway.

I tighten my grip on the switchblade.

"I accept," I say. "Five-finger fillet, then?"

"The best game ever invented," Laserbeams says happily. "Just put your hand on the pedestal, and I'll sing the song, and you touch the tip of the knife to the spaces between your fingers to the beat. One and two and three and four. You win if you get through the whole song without cutting your fingers. Not even one little nick. But if you cut yourself at all, you lose. Understand?"

I stare at the outline of the hand and the four white dots on the pedestal. I vaguely remember someone doing this before, in the cafeteria during lunch, but with a plastic fork instead of a knife, breaking tines off until only one remained, and slicing it back and forth over his bandaged fingers. He wore the bandages like he was proud of his injuries, or maybe just happy that they made everyone look at him. He played obsessively, every day. He wasn't always alone. He had friends who played games with him. I can't remember his name, or his face. I can only see him there on the peripheral of my memories.

I take a breath and flatten my hand on the pedestal.

.25......

After the show.

The empty gym.

The artists and Mrs. Anderson worked together to take down the gallery and store the pieces in the art room so that Mrs. Anderson could photograph them for the scholarship program. She was beaming when I left; apparently all those rich people who gave our school money had been very impressed. Some of them had even asked if they could buy the paintings that had been on display, including mine.

Mom and Dad came to pick me up. On the way home, Mom asked, When will I get to see the greatness I inspired?

Soon, I said, laughing at her wide-eyed expression and splayed hands.

It had better be, Dad said, a smile curling at the corner of his mouth. If she doesn't get to see it soon, she's likely to start using her pruning shears on both of *us*.

The next day, I got to art class early. Mrs. Anderson was standing by the cubbies, looking stricken.

Oh, Cat, she said. I'm so sorry.

I hurried forward and checked my cubby. It was empty except for a few paintbrushes and an old rag.

I came in this morning and it was gone, she said.

Gone? What do you mean?

I thought I locked the door last night after the show, she said. I know I did. But when I got here this morning it was—it was gone. You didn't take it home, did you? Did you move it to another cubby or to a corner somewhere?

No, I said. My throat constricted, my voice rising. No, I didn't take it home. I didn't put it anywhere. Did someone come in after we left? Did they move it? When did you lock the door? Did anyone else have a key?

No—just the custodians, but they weren't here last night—no, I am the only one with the key.

We checked the art room from top to bottom. We checked the art storage room, right next door. I prayed someone had moved it. Put it under a sheet, stacked other paintings on top of it, I didn't care what they had done with it, as long as it was here. We didn't even have pictures of it to submit to the scholarship program. We had nothing.

I kept searching with the help of some of the other art students, but I knew it was gone. Months of work, gone. I tried to console myself by thinking that I could do it again, because I'd already done it once. I had the skill, and no one could steal my talent. But the creation of that painting had been something special. It wasn't just about talent or skill; it was about the emotion of making it, and the small moments all piled on top of each other. I couldn't recreate that painting, because that emotion, those moments, were gone.

It vanished? Jeffrey said at the end of the day, as we stood by our lockers. How? Who took it?

I don't know, I said. My face felt numb. My lips felt numb. Everything felt numb except my heart and my brain, which were on fire. I don't know what to do. I can't paint it again, I said. Not like it was, and not in time to submit for the scholarship.

He frowned. We'll figure something out, he said. There must be some way to find out who took it. We'll go to administration if we have to.

Thanks, I said.

We should go today, he said. As soon as possible.

I wanted to curl into a ball inside my locker and stay

there until I rotted. I wanted Mrs. Anderson to deal with this mess. But I let him pull me along anyway.

The main hallway wasn't empty like it was supposed to be. School was out; people were supposed to be at sports or clubs or wherever else they went when they escaped this place. But there was a crowd gathered near the administration offices, by the cases where the trophies were displayed. Someone had cleaned out a display case and arranged a black cloth in it. A large oil painting rested against the cloth, just visible over the tops of heads.

Jeffrey had a hold of my arm; I ripped it from him and barreled into the crowd, shoving people out of the way, pushing to the front, not caring or hearing what anyone said, if they said anything at all.

It was the same as it had been last night. All except for the spray paint, and the Sharpie, and the orange-brown burn marks. Laughter filled my ears. The spray paint— the trees on fire, the stupid mustache and googly eyes— the *thing* they had drawn by my mother's face, the fucking horrible *monstrosity*—and the words *by Kitty Cat* below that, like a child had gotten hold of it—the *Sharpie*—

I grabbed the display case door and pulled and pulled until the screws in the lock popped. I pulled my painting out. A space opened around me as I fell to my knees with the canvas in my lap to rub at the paint and Sharpie with my fingers, with my shirt. It wouldn't come off.

It wouldn't come off.

Cat.

Jeffrey kneeled next to me.

Cat! Stop!

He grabbed my hands. I looked up. Everyone had disappeared. Mrs. Anderson, Principal Mitchell, and Vice Principal Kaur stood over us.

They ruined it! I yelled. They fucking ruined it!

Who ruined it? Principal Mitchell asked.

Jake and his fucking stupid friends!

Please watch your language, said Vice Principal Kaur.

Who else would sign it *by Kitty Cat*? They'd drawn a dick on my mom's face and given her fucking googly eyes and set her trees on fire. Then they displayed it for everyone to see. For *me* to see. They wanted me to have it back.

Jeffrey pulled me up off the floor and Mrs. Anderson tried to take the painting out of my hands. I ripped it away from her and held it to my chest.

We'll need that, the principal said. If we're going to get to the bottom of this.

You'll never get to the bottom of this, I wanted to say. *You'll never get to the bottom because none of them will ever admit what they did, and you won't care enough to try. They'll never tell you how awful they are. And neither will anyone else.*

Come on, Cat, Jeffrey said, gently working the painting from my rigid fingers.

There's nothing you can do.

NOTHING YOU CAN DO

The song starts slow.

I don't hear the words. I focus on my knife hitting the little white dots between my spread fingers. All I need is a rhythm. Even once it gets fast, as long as I have a rhythm, I can win.

He speeds up gradually.

Tap   tap   tap   tap

goes the knife between my fingers. My grip is loose, just tight enough to keep my switchblade on point. I am good at this. I can do this. I am precise, I am calm, I am patient.

I am a cat.

The song speeds up; he reaches a bridge. It's almost over. It has to be almost over, unless he's going to keep going forever. *Tap tap tap   tap*. Stay relaxed. Even. With the beat.

The final chorus is faster. My arm jackhammers back and forth. The breeze from the knife skims the top of my fingers.

I will not cut myself.

I will not lose.

It's almost over.

onetwothreefour

taptaptaptap

This must be the final chorus.

Breath fans the back of my neck.

Breathnotwind

A hand comes down on top of my knife and forces the blade to the left.

Slicing my ring finger clean off.

.26......

Principal Mitchell had listened to my story and said he'd get to the bottom of it, but I knew he wouldn't do anything. He wouldn't do anything to Jake, star of the school, straight-A athlete, loved by everyone who mattered. The principal said whatever he had to say to get me to shut up. Nobody liked the weird girl in the black turtleneck whining about her ruined picture.

Jeffrey sat next to me on the bleachers in his button-up shirt, sleeves rolled to his elbows. He'd given me his sweater vest to hold, because it was soft and the detergent smell of it calmed me down. He kept his elbows on his knees and his hands folded carefully together.

What am I going to do? I said. I don't—I don't have

anything anymore. Why do they have to take everything away? Why do they have to ruin *everything*?

I don't know, Jeffrey said.

When did Jake get like this? When did he become such an asshole?

When our dad left, Jeffrey said. But that's not an excuse.

I buried my face in the sweater vest. The material was soft against my skin, like fur.

I hate them, I mumbled again.

Jeffrey put an arm around my shoulders and held me close to his side. He pressed his face into my hair.

I'm sorry, he said.

We sat there until the sun went down. He drove me to my house, where I reluctantly returned his sweater vest, and then he made sure I was calm before he handed me my keys.

Text me later, okay? he said. Or call me. Whatever you want. Just let me know you're okay.

It was already dark. My parents were used to me being late, so when I walked through the kitchen, Mom didn't look up from her pruning when she said hello and asked how my day had been. I pulled leftover lasagna out of the fridge and started making myself a dinner I didn't plan to eat.

Weren't you supposed to bring that painting home? Mom said from behind me, voice eager. Where is it? When can I see?

My hand froze on the microwave handle. I bit my lip, then said, Mrs. Anderson's still taking photos for the scholarship people.

Oh, but I thought I'd get to see it!

Sorry, Mom.

Well . . . as long as you get the scholarship, I suppose it will be worth it.

I walked out of the room and left my dinner behind.

FUNSIES

I drop the switchblade and fall away from the pedestal, gasping for air and grasping for reality. My finger stays where it is.

"Jesus—Jesus, my finger—"

"Another one for me!"

The hand that shoved mine plucks my finger from the pedestal. The body the hand is attached to groans and wheezes as it straightens up, and with horror I recognize the matted yellow fur and pizza grease stains, the shark-toothed jaw and empty eye socket. His legs wobble, and he's missing an arm and part of his face. Hot pizza cheese bubbles slowly from a rip in his abdomen. Mark turns, bearing down on me.

Wrapped around his broken neck are two small legs in black pants. Gripping his empty eye sockets are two little hands in white gloves. The doll that clings to his head is hidden behind him. Mark's mouth falls open on its hinge.

"This is a nice change. Most of the fingers I get are dead," he says in that high-pitched, cracking voice.

I scramble back, holding my hand to my chest. I don't know how to stop the blood; I need to stop the blood.

"Where are you going, Cat?" he asks. "You lost. Don't you remember?" He wags my finger at me. "That means you have to stay here."

I dig my heels in and push myself away from him.

He follows, one jerky step at a time. Loose fur and trails of pink, pulsing innards hang from his body.

"Uh-uh," Laserbeams says. "Bad kitty."

With a gust of air, one of the knives detaches from the ceiling and lodges into the floor behind me. My back flattens against its cold, smooth steel.

"What are you?" My voice shakes.

The doll holding on to Mark's head edges into view. It's a boy wearing a too-big tuxedo. The sleeves are bunched up around his elbows, the collar gaping wide around his wooden neck. His brown hair is combed neatly to the side above his wide, round blue eyes. His mouth has been sectioned off to move independently up and down.

A ventriloquist dummy, like in a bad B horror movie.

Strung around his neck is a row of human fingers on a fishing line—at least ten of them. He stares at me intensely. I imagine little red pinpricks of light, like red rifle sights locked on my forehead.

"I haven't found a good body in ages," Laserbeams says. The voice belongs to the puppet, but it comes out of Mark's mouth. "Most people fight too hard, and they get all beaten up, but you came right in here! So what do you say, pal? Want to give me a real ride to cruise around in? I'd like to know what it's like to always land on my feet. *Meow.*"

I reach behind me and use the big knife to push myself up, but I grab the blade edge by mistake. A bright flash of pain sears my palm. Now both hands are bleeding.

"You're ruining it!" Laserbeams cries. "Stop doing that! One finger is just for funsies, but if you go around cutting yourself, you're going to turn out as badly as Mark!"

I am glued to the spot. If I move, another knife might plummet from above, and this time it might actually hit me.

I have to get out of here.

"It's going to hurt a lot more if you resist. Just saying."

The edges of the room brighten. There are hundreds upon hundreds of knives overhead. The walls—the walls aren't that far away from us at all. And piled against them, on both sides of me, for as far as I can see, are bodies. Broken bodies. Bloody bodies. I don't recognize anyone, but they must have been students.

"If I had a penny for every scream . . . I mean, really, Julie

Wisnowski?" He motions to the pile of corpses to his left, to the pieces of her porcelain body. "That girl had lungs. Even Mark screamed, and I didn't think he still could."

I jump to my feet and run. Toward the dark throat that will lead back to the boys' restroom.

Laserbeams groans. "*No, don't do that!*"

The doors of this white room swing shut. I slam into them, fingers scrabbling against the smoothness, leaving trails of blood.

Shunk

Shunk

Shunk

Knives fall from the ceiling like shot birds. Some clatter harmlessly and others lodge in the floor. One after another after another down down down down until the floor is a minefield. Laserbeams stands in the center of the room and knives fall around him. One topples over close to me. I grab the huge wooden handle and hold the blade flat over my head like a shield. Two knives above me fall, hit it, and glance off.

"Stop it!" I yell.

"And they said *I* was a slow learner." Laserbeams shuffles closer. One of Mark's knees gives out, and he stumbles, then regains his footing. I cower beneath my shield with nine fingers and no way out of this place. I could use this knife as a weapon— swing it at him, try to destroy his legs to stop him from moving— but what if there are more knives I can't see? What if I move this one and a new one splits my skull? I don't know what else Laserbeams controls, and I don't want to find out.

I want to go home. I want to be curled up under my covers with my sketchbooks and Mom working on her trees in the next room and Dad watching tennis matches on the TV and my phone vibrating with Jeffrey's name on the screen. Surely whatever happened can't be as bad as this place.

"Did you hear that?" Laserbeams asks.

I freeze, hold my breath. Is this another game?

Then I hear it, too. Distant voices echoing.

" . . . knew we should have left you. This is ridiculous."

"Sorry, not all of us have completely functional limbs."

"What cardboard god did you piss off to—wait, what the hell? Why is the door closed?"

"HELP!" I drop my knife and bang against the door. "GET IT OPEN!"

Laserbeams snarls. "No, don't—don't do—"

"Stand back!" someone yells from the other side.

I find an opening and run for it, feet sliding. Laserbeams tries to follow me but gets stuck in his own maze; Mark's body doesn't handle well. I dive behind a knife and brace myself against it.

The door explodes inward.

.27......

It's my fault.

It's not your fault.

I should have known he would do something like that.

With what? Your psychic powers?

I'm his brother. That's basically psychic.

It's not your fault. There was nothing you could have done. If it's anyone fault, it's mine. I should have told Mrs. Anderson I could take pictures of it myself, and I should have brought it home that night. But I didn't, and it's too late now.

He's a dick.

Yeah, I know.

He's a DICK.

Jeffrey, I got it the first time.

I know. He's in the next room, I wanted him to hear.

Oh. Well, good.

Are you going to be okay tonight?

I'll be fine.

Call me if you need anything.

I will.

I'm sorry.

Me, too. See you in the morning.

Night, Cat.

Night.

BLOOP BLOOP

When the dust clears, all the knives are flat on the floor, except the one I'm holding. Time and his Hands stand in the doorway, flanked by the two huge Saint Bernards.

Still stuffed, but also mobile. And growling like the engines of Satan's motorcycle gang.

"Hey, Laserfuck," Time says. "Hand over my fingers."

Mark's body, knocked over by the blast, lays immobile. Then his head lifts, and Laserbeams peeks out from behind it.

"Ugh," he says.

Time smiles.

"Cat!"

Jeffrey climbs past one of the Saint Bernards and falls across the knives. I dart out and meet him halfway before he collapses for good.

"What are you doing here?" I ask. "You're—you're walking! Why are you here?"

"Loverboy comes to me like five minutes after you leave, asking where you are," Time says. He has his arms folded across his chest, but the Hands all have weapons. "Says, '*Oh, Cat's gone, where did Cat go, why isn't Cat here,*' and won't goddamn leave until I tell him. *Then* he insists we come after you, because he's *so* certain you're dying, or something, and he says it's *my* responsibility to get my own fingers back, which is honestly bullshit. This guy's a freaking fly, Cat Lady; why haven't you ditched him yet?"

I look at Jeffrey, but he's busy examining my hands.

"Cat . . . what happened? What did he do?"

"He's the killer," I say. "Laserbeams killed Julie and Mark and the others—he's killing everyone, Jeffrey, just look." I point to the walls. Jeffrey looks, focusing on his surroundings for the first time. His boxhands curl around my elbows.

"It'll be okay," he says. "Time will take care of it."

Time marches across the knife-strewn floor with the Saint Bernards on his heels. Laserbeams struggles to sit up, but the explosion blew off one of Mark's legs and severed his waist halfway. The four Hands fan out to either side, and they and Time and the dogs create a ring around Mark's body.

"Any last words?" Time asks. "Anything you want to apologize for?"

"Go eat some curry," Laserbeams says.

Time smiles and makes a circle in the air with a finger. "Fuck him up!"

The Hands attack. All I see from where Jeffrey and I sit is the circle of legs and Mark's broken body between them, being smashed and speared and torn. Sledgehammers, swords, huge jaw-like things that rip fur from flesh and crunch through bone. Mark's body jerks back and forth, beaten and abused beyond death. The Hands smile as they perform their work; Laserbeams isn't the only one who enjoys inflicting pain. Time watches it all impassively.

I don't want to watch. I don't want to see any more beatings or stabbings or destruction, and I don't want to see anyone taking joy in it. I can't stand it. But I also can't look away. There's something in my brain that says, *Look, look, look what can happen, look what can be inflicted on another human, by humans. Look how we can be undone.* Jeffrey tries to pull me closer, but he can hardly keep his hands around my arms.

When the Hands finish, Time says, "Macaroni. Forte."

The dogs spring forward. Growling, they rip what's left of Mark apart and toss the pieces to either side of the room. Just like that, he is gone forever, another one of the discarded.

I pull Jeffrey to his feet and we move toward the door. The sooner we get out of here, the better. Laserbeams is done. He won't be killing anyone else. Now he is only himself, a ventriloquist dummy in an oversized tuxedo, harmless amid the knives.

"Why don't they kill him, too?" Jeffrey whispers.

"I think he's useless without a body," I say.

Time uses the tip of a knife to slice the string of fingers off of Laserbeams's neck and lift it away from him. Time finds his own fingers, discards the others. He removes his glove, then takes a crude needle attached to a spool of thread from his pocket. He begins stitching his middle finger back on.

"Doing this one first so I can flip you off properly," he says.

"Should we smash his head or something?" one of the Hands asks.

Time scoffs. "Shut the fuck up, Tod."

He stabs the needle back into his finger, and there's a blur of movement on the floor. A crack splits the air. Laserbeams's legs are wrapped around Time's neck and his fingers scrabble through Time's hair, over his face, searching for something.

Time's hands twitch upward. His legs buckle.

Laserbeams's fingers smash through the lenses of Time's Wayfarers and pop his eyes.

.28. . . . . .

Summer.

The summer after.

I hid on the back deck among the bonsai and stared up at the sky. Sunny days, cloudy days, didn't matter.

Sometimes I tried drawing the gentle curve of a trunk or a tangle of branches, but my pencil always felt dull, the paper thin, and my patience nonexistent. My sketchbooks gathered dust. I worked in the nursery and taught people how to get started with their own beginner's bonsai kits. Mom asked once a day if I'd heard about the scholarship. Once a day, I said no.

Eventually I would have to say they rejected me. I would never tell her what really happened.

The painting was under a sheet in my cubby in the art room. The investigation into the incident had, unsurprisingly, gone nowhere. If you turned in someone like Jake, you ended up like me—harassed and ridiculed for the rest of eternity. If you found something to relieve you of their harassment, they took that away, too. I couldn't pick up a pencil without a crushing weight landing on my shoulders.

What have you eaten today? Jeffrey asked me one day as we took a walk around his neighborhood. If we hung out there when Jake was home, we were always *near* his house, never inside it.

I don't know, I said, rubbing a hand over my stomach absently. I think I had a granola bar for breakfast. Or . . . maybe that was yesterday.

Are you sure you're eating enough?

I'm not dead, am I?

He gave me an *Are we really playing like this?* look and tucked his hands into the pockets of his cargo shorts. He wore typical Jeffrey during-the-summer garb: shorts, sandals, T-shirt with a logo of a tropical beach bar I'd never heard of. As far as I knew he'd never been to any tropical beach bars, but his mom definitely had; she spent every minute she could telling stories about her wild college spring breaks.

It was too hot for long sleeves and pants, so I had broken out a dress again. I only really felt okay wearing a dress when

I was hanging out with Jeffrey, because I knew he wouldn't point out how weird it was that I was wearing a dress. This one in particular was the one I'd worn the first time I'd gone over to his house years ago, but it felt too big now. I pulled it tighter and realized my hipbones and ribs stuck out.

Jesus, Cat, Jeffrey said, stopping as soon as he saw me. We're getting you food right now. Where do you want to go? McDonald's? IHOP? Somewhere with more calories?

I'm okay, I said. I'm really not hungry.

When was the last time you had an actual meal?

I thought about it. Mom always filled up my plate at dinner, but she never seemed to notice that I only nibbled on most of it. Dad wasn't much of an eater, either.

I don't know, I said.

Jeffrey dragged me back to my house and forced me to drive us to IHOP, where we split the biggest breakfast they had. Jeffrey shot his straw wrapper at me and poured all the syrup on my side of the plate. I told him for every bite he ate, I'd eat one. He ate more than I'd ever seen him eat, and my stomach threatened to burst.

On the drive back to his house, he said, Promise me you'll eat dinner tonight. And breakfast tomorrow morning.

If my stomach doesn't explode, I said.

Cat, seriously.

I promise.

Thank you.

He ran his hands through his hair and rested his forehead on his window. I found his hand and squeezed it.

Only one more year, he said. Then Jake goes to college on the other side of the country, and we can forget about this.

Yeah, I said. It'll be nice.

NEW GAME

"**G**et him OFF OF ME!" Time's hands scrabble against Laserbeams, upsetting the doll's hair and catching in the giant collar of his tuxedo, but Laserbeams is immovable. Time stumbles across the floor, trips on the pedestal stained with my blood, and falls on the knives. Laserbeams still has his hands in Time's eye sockets; blood pours down Time's face, stains his pretty white teeth. "Get this motherfucker off of me right now!"

"Just give up, you stupid bitch! Let me have your body!" Time's voice cranks higher.

"Go fuck yourself!" he says like his normal self.

Time and Laserbeams wobble around the room. The Hands glance at one another, weapons at the ready. Macaroni and Forte growl and whine.

I pull Jeffrey toward the remains of the door. "We need to go."

"You were stupid enough to get that close to me!" Laserbeams screams. "You don't deserve this body!"

"It's *mine*—" Time's body goes rigid. Slowly—first his shoulders, then his arms, all the way down to his feet—he begins to relax. Laserbeams still clings to his head and neck. Time, like some kind of ragdoll, slumps over at the waist, his back to us. His hands search the ground, find the handle of one of the big knives.

Then, quick as lightning, he snaps upward, spins, and hurls the knife at us. It slams into Forte's chest, sending the dog flying into the wall where he hangs, pinned. Macaroni lets out a monstrous bark and lunges at Time. Time waits for the dog to get close, then grabs him by the neck. His fingers tear Macaroni open, and cloudy stuffing bursts from the torn seam. Macaroni goes limp.

Time picks up a massive kitchen knife and turns to the Hands.

The Hands charge, weapons raised. With a few quick, clean slices, two of them lose their legs. The third gets his head— *shick*—separated from his shoulders. *No more, no more, no more,* I think. And poor Tod, who tries to back away at the last second, gets the kitchen knife shoved into his chest and cranked around like a key in a lock.

"Run!" I shove Jeffrey toward the dark tunnel.

"I'm not going to leave you here!" he says. He doesn't let go of my arm, and I have to peel his fingers off.

"Go warn the others," I say. "Please, Jeffrey. I can hold him off, at least for a little while. You have to go warn the others!"

"He has a body; why would he need to kill us now?"

"Yes, Cat, why would I need to kill you?" Laserbeams's voice is clear and high-pitched and it's coming out of Time's mouth. "I just want to be friends. Honest."

"Go, Jeffrey!" I give him one more shove, and he relents, swinging around and crab walking toward the staircase on his hands and feet.

I turn back. Laserbeams, paused several feet from me, waits patiently. The Wayfarers are still on Time's face, smashed and bent and held in place by Laserbeams. I notice for the first time that his little doll hands are *not* wearing white gloves, like I thought— they're wrapped in bandages. He raises the knife and points at the staircase.

"Wanna play another game?" Laserbeams asks. "I bet I can kill Jeffrey before he warns anyone what happened here."

I wrench a knife out of the floor. I am strong, and I am fast, and I have to do this now to make sure he will never hurt Jeffrey.

"Fuck you," I say.

His knife comes down hard. I block it with my own. He springs back, then forward again, slashing at my side. I block again. He moves the giant kitchen knife faster and more fluidly than a giant kitchen knife should be able to move, but when I try, I discover I can move mine just as well.

The lights in the room dim. The bodies along the walls

disappear. We swing the knives so quickly they're blurs in the dark, defying the laws of physics. The clang of steel on steel echoes through the room. I attack, aiming for his legs. Time's too nimble. Laserbeams isn't controlling slow, clunky Mark anymore.

My hands begin to ache. They are covered in blood. I am missing a finger and my palm is sliced open. Only when I remember that does the handle of the knife slip, and Time's next strike sends it sailing. He flips his knife on its side and smacks me with the flat of the blade. The room blurs; I crash against the wall and roll down the dark pile of bodies.

"I'll leave you alive," he says. "Want to make sure you see my victory."

He sprints for the stairs.

Head spinning, I push myself to my feet and run after him.

.29......

Something is going to happen to Jeffrey.

Something happened to Jeffrey that summer.

We are juniors now.

I mean, it was technically normal. Boys keep growing after girls stop, whatever. But one day I looked at him and *bam*, different face. *His* face, but he'd finally grown into it. It had finished that rearranging process it had started freshman year.

The honeypillar eyebrows weren't really honeypillars anymore. His face fit them now, so instead of blond caterpillars above his eyes, he had two stern shelves that all his emotions rested upon. He was an unflappable steel wall, and those eyebrows were the first line of defense. Even Jake, with his bright green eyes and athletic tan and dimpled smile, couldn't compete.

On the first day of junior year, I stood with Jeffrey at his locker, watching him work on memorizing his combination. His nearness helped my neck stop prickling whenever a senior was near. He mouthed the numbers as he spun the dial. Frowned when the tab wouldn't go up and open the door. Tried it again.

Did you take something? I asked.

He glanced sideways at me. What?

Did you take something? Or get an injection? Did a mad scientist strap you down to a table and operate on you?

He laughed. What are you talking about?

I'm talking about *this*. I motioned to all of him. When did this happen, and why wasn't I informed?

He gave up on his locker completely.

Okay, you're freaking me out now, he said. Explain.

Have you looked in a mirror today? I asked.

I did.

So can you tell me why someone kidnapped my best friend and replaced him with the hotness?

The *hotness*? Jeffrey frowned. Then a smile took over his face, crinkling his eyes. He lifted his chin and puffed out his chest. You think I'm hot?

I never said that.

You think I'm hot.

I didn't—

You think *I'm* hot.

Nope—

You think I'm *hot*.

Jeffrey, I swear to God—

He gently flicked my nose.

Now we can be hot together, he said.

I blushed. What?

Sorry, probably should have told you that sooner.

I hesitated. Was he just saying that so I didn't feel awkward? Because he wanted to be a good friend? Was this playing, or serious?

Cat, he said. You're worrying.

I'm not.

I know your face when you're worrying.

So?

No one's ever said I looked hot before, he said. It's kind of nice, you know?

You don't have to say it back just so I don't feel left out. I'm fine.

I *didn't* say it so you don't feel left out.

Then why'd you say it?

'Cause . . . that's what I really think.

Geez, you don't have to lie to me.

Cat, come on, I don't want this to get weird.

Weird in what way?

Cat.

Weird in what way?

He covered his face with his hands and groaned. I'm not doing this right now, he said. Not in the hallway.

I had to know. If Jeffrey wormed his way out of this, I would never know exactly what he was talking about. He'd never bring it up again.

Where, then? I asked. The art storage room is empty during lunch. Does that work? Then can you tell me why this is weird?

He peeked at me through his fingers. You have to know that badly?

Judging by the way you're acting, yeah, I do.

I kept my expression calm and pressed my palms to my thighs so my jeans could soak up the sweat.

Fine, he said. Fine, I'll tell you at lunch. Just stop looking at me like that.

I stopped looking at him like that.

My first four classes of the day were slower than even I could've imagined. My teachers basically all knew me thanks to the painting bullshit last year, and they didn't seem to mind that I didn't pay attention. I was trying to draw the swoop of Jeffrey's hair in the margins of my notebooks, but it wasn't working well.

When the bell rang for lunch, I found Jeffrey waiting for me outside the cafeteria.

Let's get this over with, he said, and then he clammed up. His eyebrows became those stern shelves. He usually had a pretty hard-to-crack exterior, but he was rarely so quiet and unyielding. I led him to the storage room adjacent to the art classroom. Most of the art students knew this as Mrs. Anderson's abandoned photography studio. It was once used for photo shoots when the school offered photography classes but had been cluttered up with extra art supplies more recently. What resulted was a small room packed with old storage shelves up to the ceiling, and random pieces of furniture stuffed in between: a green armchair, a screen for changing in privacy, and a divan that looked like it had been chewed by a dog. I checked to make sure no one else was inside, pulled the curtain over the window in the door, then locked the door behind us.

Okay, I said. Let's hear it.

You didn't have to lock the door, Jeffrey said.

Are you afraid I'm going to eat you?

Of course not.

He tucked his hands into his pockets.

I like you, he finally said. His face shone red.

A strange feeling rippled under my skin, but I didn't have time to identify it beyond the fact that it made my tongue numb.

Since when? I asked.

He shrugged. Eighth grade, maybe.

Why didn't you tell me?

I didn't want it to get weird, he said. We're best friends. I thought if I told you, it would ruin that. Again. We already spent a whole semester not talking to each other. I don't want to not talk to you for the rest of my life.

So when you found out I liked Jake . . . you were jealous?

Well, yeah. But mostly worried, because I know what kind of person Jake is, and I know he doesn't care about people like us.

People like us?

People . . . beneath him.

People in the river, I thought. *People just trying to make it to the sea.*

I guess you were right, I said.

I'm not happy about it. He tapped his heel against the floor, as if trying to get his shoe to fit better. So . . . are we okay? I don't expect anything from you, but now that you know, I'm going to be worrying all the time if you think I'm trying to get with you.

I twisted the sleeve of my shirt around my fingers. Was I okay with Jeffrey liking me? I'd been okay with it for the past three years, even though I hadn't known about it. Jeffrey had never been anything but my friend.

What if you liked him, too?

The question set loose heat in my stomach. I had never really allowed myself to consider the idea; it seemed almost taboo. Even if he was reliable and caring and smart and handsome and made me laugh, he was Jeffrey. But he'd knocked on the door; all I had to do was open it.

I balled my shirtsleeves around my hands and stepped closer to him. He straightened up. Another step, and we were toe-to-toe. I tapped my sleeve-covered hand on his chest.

I like your sweater vests, I said.

I like your paintings, he said. Especially the weird ones.

I gently punched him.

He flicked my nose.

I grabbed his ears and pulled him down to kiss him.

EXHALE

School is exhaling. School is exhaling *hard.*

The hallways are contracting even as I run through them, growing brighter and brighter. I sprint between the lockers. No matter how bright it gets, the hallways in front of me and behind me always stay black as night.

I run faster than I ever have before, faster than anyone I know, but Time runs faster. Even though I am sure I was only a few steps behind, I don't see Time on the stairs, or in the boys' bathroom, or in the hallways. I hear his annoying, high-pitched laughter everywhere, and I push myself faster.

Maybe Jeffrey took another route to the Fountain Room.

Maybe Laserbeams doesn't know his way around up here.

Maybe Jeffrey has already gotten there, and everyone had time to hide.

It'll be like when I found him in Mrs. Remley's room. He's just hiding. He's too smart to get caught.

The hallways back to the Fountain Room are winding and endless, but eventually I reach it. I charge through the doorway and sprint around the north fountain.

Laserbeams isn't here.

Neither is anyone else.

The little colony of tents and pillows and blankets and supplies has been ransacked. There is nothing standing. I creep closer. The fountains explode upward toward the lowering ceiling. They're not shooting water anymore; they're shooting blood, like the showers in the girls' locker room. And because School is exhaling, the fountains are flooding the room. With blood.

I creep toward the remains of Sissy's tent and realize Jeffrey did make it here after all.

Why why why now.

I don't want this to hurt worse than it already does.

I did get to make out at school.

Most days Jeffrey and I took our lunches to the storage room. Some days we snuck in and everything was great. Other days we had to wait for a distraction—like Ken Kapoor starting a food fight in the cafeteria by chucking bits of bean burrito at Ryan Lancaster where he sat at his table with his broken plastic utensils and few friends, who tried to throw back but never succeeded in hitting Ken—to get inside the storage room without anyone seeing us. And some days there were just too many people around, so we ate with everyone else and acted like nothing had changed.

Everything had changed.

I was drawing again. I ate three meals a day. I picked up a brush and started working on another painting to send to the scholarship foundation, because even though I knew it would never be as good as the ruined picture of Mom and her bonsai, I remembered that I had enough talent to get my foot in the door. My grades stabilized somewhat, too, but I was more concerned with running my hands through Jeffrey's hair.

We kept our meetings a secret not for any real reason other than we enjoyed not having to explain ourselves to anyone.

I honestly don't care if Jake or anyone finds out about this, I said one day in late September as we laid on the divan, an assortment of lunch foods spread out around us. Jeffrey was busy plucking grapes from a bunch and stuffing them into his cheeks.

Me, either, he mumbled. Screw those guys.

They can keep speculating on my sexuality, I said.

None of their business anyway, he said.

I leaned over and kissed him on the cheek. He grinned.

Being with him was easy. As easy as it had been before, or maybe easier, since neither of us was holding anything back. Friends but more. Friends Plus. The *Jeffrey Blumenthal's Best Friend* brand on my forehead had never changed. I just started appreciating it again.

Look, I said to him one day in October, while I sat in an armchair and he relaxed on the divan, posing for me. I turned my sketchbook toward him.

You're going to color me in, right? he said.

Of course I'm going to color you in.

Whatever happened to that picture of Jake you did?

Burned it, I said.

Really?

No, I tore it out and threw it away. But I burned it in my heart.

Good enough.

I moved over to sit next to him.

How are you going to do a picture of me from that close? he asked.

I'm getting the details, I said.

What details? My giant nose?

Your nose is perfect. I'm talking about stuff like . . . the hairs in your eyebrows.

Do people look that closely at portraits?

No. I just really like your eyebrows.

In that case, have some.

He leaned forward and pressed his forehead to my cheek. I laughed and pushed him away.

It didn't take too long before we expanded our territory. When I told my parents we were together, Dad wanted Jeffrey over for dinner at least once a week, and Mom applauded his clean appearance and organizational skills and assaulted him with questions about college and careers every time he sat down at our table. We still only went into his house when Jake wasn't home, and even then, we stayed secluded in Jeffrey's bedroom. We spent hours on his bed eating Skittles and watching terrible horror movies, and I found out how well I fit into the curve of his arm.

One day in November, I moved Skittles into color-specific piles on his chest while a murderer chopped away at teenagers having sex onscreen.

Doesn't even make sense, Jeffrey said. He's not exactly quiet. They would have heard him coming.

Too busy listening to each other coming, I said.

Jeffrey coughed so hard he dislodged the Skittles.

Could you be more vulgar? he said.

Actually, yes, I could. It's just the truth. Who's going to notice an ax murderer sneaking up on you when you're in the throes of passionate sex in a dirty, disease-ridden barn? If you're horny enough to get it on in there, you're not going to notice *anything*.

Jeffrey wriggled against my side. Now he watched a piece of wall slightly above the small television. I sat up and leaned over him to pick up the Skittles that had fallen on the comforter. His hands held my hips.

Don't hover over me like that, he said.

Oh, sorry, am I blocking the TV?

He lunged upward, caught my lips, locked his arms around my waist, and pulled me back down with him. I gave up on the Skittles. We curled together on his bed until the front door slammed shut and jolted us apart. Heavy footsteps thudded down the hallway.

Guess who's home? Jeffrey said. He turned his head and stifled a groan into his pillow.

Don't worry, I said. We can pick this back up on Monday.

I never got tired of going to school or looking for new ways to sneak into the storage room. It was a place to hide from threats patrolling the halls, like Jake or his friends. The painting I was doing for the scholarship wasn't great, but it was good, and I didn't care much either way how it ended up. Maybe if I took it easy, it would become easy, like the last one. Jeffrey pushed me to work on it every day, even when I pouted and whined, even when it felt like I was tearing my fingernails out. My reward for getting work done was always an afternoon in the storage room.

So one day in December, while some of the other art students were still working on projects, but I'd finished a difficult section of my new painting—my own hand holding the paintbrush, painting myself into infinity—Jeffrey and I locked ourselves in the storage room and fell over on the divan like it was our job. My need to touch him felt more urgent today, like his lips and hands weren't enough. Plus he was wearing a new burgundy sweater vest that made him look sexy as hell, and I told him so as I pulled it off over his head.

Untuck your shirt, I told him.

Why?

Because I want to know what you look like with an untucked shirt.

He did.

Hot, I said.

He smiled and leaned in for my lips again, but I ducked him and went for his neck.

Are you feeling okay? he asked.

I feel great, I said. I started unbuttoning his shirt. He grabbed my hands.

What are we doing right now?

What do you *want* to be doing right now?

I can think of a few things, he said.

Cool, I said. Let's do them.

At school?

I paused. Reconsidered. Said, Maybe I didn't think this through.

He stared at me. Those eyebrows hovered between uncertain and intrigued.

I want to, he said, but not here.

I sat back. Okay, I said.

Okay?

I took his face and made him look at me. You're my best friend, I said. You have been for five years. You're my best friend, and I love you, and you're totally right, it would be gross and weird to do this at school.

I love you, too, he said. I hope we're not in a horror movie.

PAINFUL HOLLOW

Jeffrey floats in bright red blood.

He is in the fountain, bumping against the side as the overflow spills onto the floor. The blood soaks into his white shirt and his khakis and his sweater vest. It seeps into his cardboard skin. His left arm has been sliced off at the elbow; the other half floats a few feet away. He's face-up; his eyes and mouth are blurs of color. There is a hole in his chest, and from it bloom red petals of blood. It stares at me, that hole. It pulls me in, an abyss of violence, a dark place my mind knows but hasn't yet shown me.

I climb into the fountain, kneel beside Jeffrey, and pull him into my arms. His head rests awkwardly over my shoulder, but I can't think of anything else to do. I can't think of anything except the way he used to smile. I can't do anything but wrap myself tighter around him, hoping he's just stunned, or unconscious, that he'll wake up again and be okay.

"Jeffrey." I cradle him and touch his face. What's left of his face. "Jeffrey, wake up. Wake up."

Blood rises above my knees, over my thighs. Something sloshes though the murk and stops behind me.

Let it be Laserbeams. Let it be Jake and his army. I don't care anymore. It doesn't matter if my memories ever tell me how we got here, or if I ever find a way out, because Jeffrey will have to stay behind.

"Cat?"

I turn to find Sissy and the others. They look at Jeffrey and then at me, and their faces are pale and their lips shut tight. Even Sissy doesn't seem to want to speak. I am used to them being scared now. I no longer care.

"What?" I snap.

"Jake and some of the administration kids came in here and destroyed our things." She motions to the stuff sinking in the blood. "He said it was too dangerous for us to have free access to the hallways. Said we'd have to be *restricted*. But then Time showed up with that puppet thing and attacked us. We got away, and so did most of the administration kids, except Shondra. . . . "

I look around. Shondra's body is half submerged in the other fountain, facedown, her hair fanning around her head. She, too, has been sliced to pieces.

"But Jeffrey wasn't here," Sissy said. "Jeffrey left to find you. . . . "

So Jeffrey had gotten here after Laserbeams; Laserbeams didn't have to chase him at all. Jeffrey wrapped himself up with a bow and said *Happy birthday, please kill me*. He didn't even know. He couldn't have known. None of us ever know.

Would it have been safer if he stayed with me? If I hadn't sent him away?

"Where did Laserbeams go?" I ask.

"Laserbeams?"

"That thing attached to Time's head," I say. "Time is dead. Laserbeams is Time now."

"I don't know where he went. We came back when we heard you."

I want them to leave me. I want to drown in this flood.

Blood encircles my waist. The room stinks of death and rot.

"We should go before Jake comes back," says West.

I hold tightly to Jeffrey I won't let him be alone.

"He's right, Cat," Sissy says. I barely hear her.

"Go without me."

"We're not going to do that." She puts her hand on my shoulder, and her tentacle slithers after it. I shake her off.

Then there comes a sharp *snap*, and someone screams. I turn as a second snap sounds, and a metal net unfurls in midair, snaring El and two others. They fall into the red lake around us, struggling to keep themselves above the surface.

snap

snap

snap

More nets shoot from the dark opening of the door. They trap one person after another. One catches Sissy when she tries to run, and submerges her for a second. When she resurfaces, she's painted completely red.

I sit frozen, watching the door. No net comes for me.

"Round them up!"

Jake steps out of the darkness, eyes burning. He grips his bat in one hand, and his other—the one that he chopped off—has been replaced with a hand carved from some smooth black substance that looks like wax.

Students from administration pour into the Fountain Room. A squad of them, led by Raph, have bazookas that shoot nets strapped across their backs. They round everyone up and drag them back to the door. Jake strides toward the other fountain; blood retreats from him like the tide pulling back. The entire room starts draining. He goes to Shondra, kneels, turns her over. Brushes bloody hair away from her face. Scoops her up in his arms and stands. He walks back to the doorway and hands her to one of the other boys from administration. Then he starts toward us. Toward me.

"Are you proud of what you've done?" he asks.

"What *I've* done?" I spit. "This is *your* fault. If you had let us in—if you hadn't made us so *weak*—none of this would have happened."

"*I* made you weak?" He laughs. "Only the truly weak blame others for their weakness."

"You'd say that about your own brother?"

Jake stares down at me with cold fury in his eyes.

"Shondra is dead because you woke up that monster. The rest of us are in permanent danger. I'm not willing to make exceptions for anyone anymore. I don't care who they are." Then he turns and yells, "Take them to the gym. It's time."

"Let go of him," he says, turning back to me.

"He's your brother," I say.

"*Let go of him.*"

"No." Jake's bat comes out of nowhere and smashes into the side of my head. Colors blur. Then I'm under blood, and my head is spinning, and even if I could tell which way was up, I couldn't get there. Something grabs my collar and drags me into the air, then tosses me across the room, onto the wet tile, where I lay, staring at the ceiling, vaguely aware that Jeffrey is no longer in my arms.

snap

A net encircles me. It's hoisted over a shoulder. Jake's shoulder.

I watch the Fountain Room recede through the holes in the net.

I see him.

There is a cardboard head and a tattered blue sweater vest.

There is a cardboard head.

There is cardboard.

There is nothing.

.31......

I let memory swallow me.

Does it matter?

Because of everything going on around school so close to the winter holidays, Jeffrey and I never found a time to go back to the storage room. Between speech team and student council, Jeffrey was busy most afternoons, and I still had my painting to finish. Mrs. Anderson said she'd give me full credit for it even though it was late, but I think she was a little afraid of me by that point.

Two weeks at home were a blessing. Time with Mom and Dad, the darkness of my room, the peace of the nursery, and the serene quiet of my mind. I texted Jeffrey and haunted social media, keeping up with the lives of my classmates where they couldn't see me. Lane Castillo had bragged about doing a home belly button piercing, but now it was badly infected. El Miller had passed out at a party, so a bunch of boys had taken the opportunity to smear her good-girl image by drawing dicks on her face and sharing pictures online. Ryan Lancaster had posted a video reading his manifesto; the comments were a bunch of jokers asking when he was going to bring his gun to school. Jake had gone skiing with a huge group of friends. I scrolled quickly past any pictures where he even threatened to appear.

After break, I spent the first day telling myself that I only had to get through five more months. Five months and Jake and his friends would be gone. I wouldn't be free from all this shit, but I'd be free from the most dangerous shit. I had Jeffrey—who hugged me tight before we parted before each class, and let me protect that soft part of himself that Jake constantly tried to attack—and I had my parents— who never tried to fix my problems, just listened to them— and I had the normal things that went on at school every day that didn't concern me—like Ken Kapoor and his goons heckling younger kids in the hallways, or Sissy and Julie in Mrs. Remley's student council room working on Julie's next campaign for presidency, or Mark sitting in the cafeteria by himself with his pizza and breadsticks.

That night, I got a text from Jeffrey:

Don't go online.

I left the rest of the dirty dishes in the sink and beelined to my laptop, my heart already racing. Jeffrey never texted me in all caps. If Jeffrey had to warn me about something, he called me. I couldn't think of anything horrible enough that he couldn't say it directly to me.

I pulled up the internet. Everything seemed fine. People were complaining about school. Raving about a burger they'd eaten for dinner. Putting up pictures of their cats.

Then I started seeing a particular video shared over and over again by people from our school, titled "I Know What You Did Last December." The thumbnail was dark, but two vaguely human outlines sat across from each other on what looked like a bed. The video was vertical, shot on a phone.

My pocket buzzed. More texts from Jeffrey. I ignored them and clicked Play on the video.

It was shot through a window in a door. The two figures, a girl and a boy, sat on a divan, one on top of the other, clothed but possibly not for long.

Ice flooded my body. I slammed down on the mouse. The video paused. The picture was dark, but not so dark you couldn't tell who we were. Anyone who went to our school would be able to tell who we were. And where we were.

I felt my pulse in my stomach and in my head.

I hadn't closed the curtain on the window that day. Neither had Jeffrey.

Someone had followed us to the door and watched.

I hit Play again. You couldn't hear us talking through the thick glass window, but when we started kissing again, sound swept in. Moaning, gasping, slick and wet sounds that made my hair stand on end. They had clipped porn audio over the video of us. It was garish, mocking. We looked awkward there on the divan, almost pitiful, like we still didn't know what to do with ourselves.

I groped for my phone. Dropped it on the floor. Picked it up and found three more texts from Jeffrey.

Cat

Are you there?

Are you okay?

I scrolled through the views, the likes, the comments. The whole school seemed to be there.

Our names were in the comments. If there was any doubt about our identities, it was gone.

And there was laughter. So much laughter. Jokes. *Memes.*

I closed the Internet and shut off the computer. How many people had watched it? A few hundred? More?

People had seen it.

Had seen *that*. With that *sound.*

It was worse than if they'd actually seen us having sex. Now it was a joke that we might even consider it. Our bodies were weird, we were weird, and the fact that we didn't realize it was the funniest joke ever told.

BLADES

I am surrounded by screams as Jake and his army drag us to the gym.

I don't want to remember anymore. I don't want to know why we're here, because I know it is a terrible thing, and I can't stand more terrible things right now.

I thrash in my net, try to pull it free from Jake's grip, but the metal mesh is sharp and tears at my fingers.

"You can't do this to us, Jake!" I yell, as if he isn't half a foot away and dragging the bloody smear of me across the floor. "We're *people*—you can't get rid of us!"

"We'll see what School has to say about that," he replies.

School's hallways are now so narrow that our procession has to march single file. Everything is bright. The only glimpses I get of the others come when I manage to twist myself around and peer ahead. I don't know where we're going.

"This is *your fault*," I hiss at Jake. "*You* did this to us. And if you kill us now, you'll have to live with what you did. Even if you *do* get out. Do you want that on you? Do you want to have such a horrible thing weighing on you for the rest of your life?"

"If I can get the others out of here," he says, "it'll be worth it."

Something cracks in the distance, followed by muffled grunting. A second later we enter the gym, and Jake tosses me beside the others at the foot of the bleachers. I straighten up, glad that the netting can't cut through my face. The others aren't having so much luck. Faces and hands have been slashed open. The netting sticks to limbs.

The gym is bright, like the hallways. The bleachers have squeezed in toward the center of the basketball court, where a wooden gallows has been erected, complete with three thick nooses. Lane Castillo stands atop the platform, wielding a spear. Raph takes up a post next to the nets. The students from administration have gathered around the gallows. I can't count them all. I know that everyone alive in School, except Laserbeams, is here now. I know it is just a fraction of the number of students that came to school before. They shuffle in place, muttering to one another, watching us, watching Jake as he jumps up to stand with Lane on the platform.

"Listen!" he yells. Silence falls over the gym. "We've been here too long. We've been scared and confused too long. We have to get out of this place before any more of us are lost to any more of *them*." He gestures to us, motionless and hopeless in our nets. "We're running out of time and we're running out of options. But we've got one plan left."

"You're making a mistake!" Pete Thompson yells.

"The Sacrifice won't work!" cries El Miller.

Jake ignores them. "If anyone has any objections, let them be known now."

No one from administration says a word. The rest of us scream, but we don't count.

"Good," Jake says. "Raph, bring the first three."

Raph moves before us with his crossbow. He motions to three nets, and several other administration boys hurry forward to collect them. Sissy is dragged from beside me. She reaches through her net to grab at mine, but Raph stomps on her wrist. She lets go.

Sissy, Pete, and a boy I remember from chemistry class are taken up to the platform and freed from their nets, and when Pete tries to run, Lane levels the tip of her spear at his throat. Raph and Lane tie their hands behind their backs and fit the nooses around their necks. Sissy is crying openly, her face red, her curly hair falling into her eyes.

I claw at my net with my bleeding fingers, looking for any way out.

"We do this not only in the hope that this sacrifice will give us a path back to our lives," Jake roars, "but to take revenge for the death of one of our own. Shondra Huston ventured into their territory with the white flag of peace, and they beat her down."

"That's *bullshit!*" Sissy spits. "She came in with the rest of you, with your weapons—you didn't give a shit that Laserbeams was killing anyone until he killed one of *you*—"

Jake pulls back the lever on the side of the gallows. The floor drops away, and Sissy's voice cuts off with a harsh choke.

I yell in hopelessness and rage, burying my face in my hands. I hear them thrashing in the open air. Blood pounds through my head, making the gym spin around me.

"Enough," Jake says. Something heavy thuds to the floor. *Thud.* I glance up in time to see them slice Sissy's rope, the blur of her falling to the gym floor. It is normal now, to see my classmates dying and dead. I am all scars.

There must be a way to get out of this net.

I wedge my remaining fingers through the netting and pull in opposite directions. The links go taut. My fingers scream in pain, but I pull harder.

"Three more," Jake yells.

Raph returns; this time he chooses one of the big nets with three of us inside, and it takes him and two other boys to get it up to the stage. The nooses are placed around the necks of El Miller and two girls who used to ride their skateboards around the middle school in the evenings.

Jake pulls the lever. I pull the net.

A link breaks. A neck snaps.

I keep pulling. Another link. I shove my foot into the newly widened hole. Push up with my hands and down with my foot.

Thud

The net begins to break away easily. Metal made of glass. Metal made of paper. Metal made of tissue.

Thud

I am rage. I am violence.

Thud

I throw the net off and turn to face the gallows.

Lane tumbles, shocked, from the platform with her own spear protruding from her chest. Those gathered at the foot of the gallows look up and scream.

Jake's feet hover a foot off the ground. Laserbeams holds him aloft by the throat. He has appeared out of nowhere, before anyone could raise an alarm. Without ceremony, he hurls Jake across the gym. Jake CRACKS against the wall and slumps to the floor.

Laserbeams turns to the crowd and spreads his arms wide. A huge knife is strapped across his back. A maniac grin stretches over Time's bloodied, eyeless face.

"Hello, friends," he says. "Let's finish what we started."

.32......

The video spread.

The number of views went up, up, up.

The night dragged on.

2:34 a.m. clicked over to *2:35 a.m.*

Both my parents were asleep.

I was glad they weren't awake now. They couldn't find out about this.

I left my laptop on my desk and sat on my bed, shaking and ill, clutching my phone in my hands. There had to be someone I could call, someone I could ask for help. My mind was blank. I couldn't ask my parents; it would kill them to know I was involved in something like this.

Six o'clock came. My alarm went off. A cheery pop song filled the room.

I couldn't go to school today.

I couldn't not go to school. My parents would think something was wrong.

I stood up to put my shoes on. My stomach lurched. I ran to the bathroom and vomited. My dad appeared in the doorway. I must have looked terrible, because he shoved me into bed and told me to stay there. Mom came up a few minutes later with a thermometer, wondering if I'd eaten something bad. I agreed I had. She checked my temperature and said she'd call school.

At some point during the day, I fell into a sort of half sleep. The faces of my classmates swam past me, whispering vulgar words, counting viewers. Laughing.

In the afternoon Mom came into my room and said, Jeffrey is here with your homework. He seems very worried. Why didn't you tell him you had food poisoning?

I pulled my blanket up like a shield before she let Jeffrey into the room. His face was pale. Not so much worried as broken completely; all the steel had been stripped out of him.

Why didn't you come to school today? he asked.

I lurched to the side of the bed to vomit into my trash can. His hands appeared to hold my hair back. It was all bile and water, and I began crying, because his touch was making my skin crawl.

I sat up, wiped my mouth, and hid my face in my blanket. I wept and he sat silent.

When I'd caught hold of myself, he said, It's not . . . it's not as bad as I thought it would be. Most people realize we were only making out, and the audio was a joke. It was clearly a joke.

I know it was, I said. But people laughed at it anyway, right? They thought it was funny, because it was us. Because no matter what changes, or who we become, we're jokes to them. We always will be.

He was silent for a moment. I wondered if he understood that part of it. That it wasn't about what we were doing, but that *we* were doing it.

I know who took the video, he said. Shondra.

Shondra?

Today, she . . . she passed me at lunch, and waved her phone at me and winked. She could have just been telling me she saw it, but it didn't feel that way.

It was possible. Shondra was often in the art wing. She could have seen us and followed us. I didn't think she hated us, but if she showed that video to Raph or Lane or, god forbid, Jake, they could have done anything.

Will they be able to tell if it was her? I asked. Would anyone be able to pin it on her?

Maybe with an IP address?

I didn't answer. At this point, did it matter if anyone got punished for it? The damage had been done.

What if it's out there forever?

It won't be out there forever.

It's the Internet. Everything is there forever.

He stared at me with hollow eyes.

Cat, he said. We didn't do anything wrong.

Do you think Jake did this? I asked.

He looked lost. Grasping for words when there were none to find. He reached out for my hand. I pulled it away from him and slipped it under the covers.

I had hoped our hesitation around each other was because we had broken up. Some misunderstanding. A mistake, like in sophomore year. Really, it was because of this.

This is what ruined us.

I COME WITH KNIVES

Laserbeams cups Time's hands around his mouth like he's going to yell, but instead a blast of blue-white fire shoots out. It lights up the edges of the gym, leaping over the doorframes. We are trapped.

We try to roll. We try to scatter.

The bleachers burn.

Laserbeams hops down from the platform, turns, and shoots another blast of fire so hot the gallows vanish in a plume of flame and ash. It sears the gym floor clear as glass. He pulls the giant kitchen knife from his back and spins it in his hands as he scans the gym.

I jump on the nearest net and begin tearing at it. I won't let us die like animals. We're better than that. We deserve more. Anger flares inside me.

"Help, help!" screams the person inside. West.

I realize he's not yelling at me, but at anyone else, at the students running past. He is yelling it *about* me.

"I *am* helping you!" I snarl at him.

I turn to and look for Laserbeams, but he's gone. No, not gone—moving too fast for me to see. Then, without warning: a girl falls to the ground. Her stomach has split open like a boiled tomato, skin peeling away, pink innards bursting.

A boy by the doors yells as his legs are cut out from under him and he topples over, his torso slamming on the glass floor. He grabs one of his ankles, motionless near his head, and screams.

Another boy is hurled skyward and slams against the rafters with a shower of sparks. He hangs there, impaled, legs and arms still jerking like a spider stuck with a tack.

One by one, they drop. Some scream before they go. Others are too scared to make a sound. Laserbeams reaches everyone eventually. Then the nets start to snap open, and the kids from the Fountain Room scramble out, only to be cut down like the administration students. West's net is yanked out of my hands by an unseen force and hurled, over and over again, against the bleachers, until the net and its contents are little more than a mangle of metal links and mashed meat.

I can do nothing to stop it. And why would I? They took Jeffrey away from me. They took everything away from me. Even their blood doesn't bother me now.

Jake was wrong. Laserbeams doesn't discriminate between the changed and the unchanged. He doesn't care who he kills.

Something grabs me by the collar and wrenches me to the floor. It's not Laserbeams, but Raph. He stands over me, his crossbow pointed at my face.

"Tell me how to stop him!" he yells.

"I don't know," I scream.

"Tell me!" he yells, planting a foot on my throat.

"I don't know how to stop him!"

I grab Raph's leg and yank it sideways. He falls but catches himself. Fires the crossbow. The bolt grazes the bridge of my nose, taking a chunk out of my mask. I flip myself over and prepare to pounce on him, to rip the crossbow away, but Laserbeams gets there first.

The knife slides through Raph's chest, easy as butter, pinning him to the floor. His eyes are wide, disbelieving, as he looks up at me. He goes limp.

Laserbeams pulls the knife out and turns to hold it in the nearby fire, letting the blood sizzle off its surface. "This was a lot of fun, Cat," he says, "I only wish it could have lasted longer."

I don't have to look around to know that everyone else is dead. It's quiet, the only sound the crackling fire. I pick up Raph's crossbow and load another bolt as quickly and quietly as I can.

"Once all of you are gone, I'm sure School will show me the way out of here," Laserbeams says. "That's what it whispered to me in the darkness. I know it spoke to you, too—didn't it tell you the same thing? Didn't it explain to you what all of this means?"

He turns back to me. I fire the crossbow.

Time falters.

I leap forward and wrench the knife from his grip.

I am a cat.

I turn the knife around and run it through Time's gut.

Dark blood gushes from his mouth.

I pull the knife out and shove it in again. And again. And again and again

until Laserbeams can no longer hold Time up, or move his legs. Until his hold on Time loosens and his doll body slips to the floor, useless. Time's head flops to the side.

Time takes a deep, shuddering breath, and says, "Thanks, Cat Lady."

Before I have even a second to think, to gain my bearings, a small hand grabs my leg. Then another. Laserbeams begins to climb me, and I try to grab him, I try to throw him off, but he's slick as an eel and as nimble as a spider. I bring my hands up to my neck before his legs wrap around it. I feel his body curving to my head, his too-big tuxedo suit crushed against my hair, his doll hands scrabbling over my mask ears, across my forehead.

"NO!" I scream, all rage, all hatred.

His hands find my eyeholes. His fingers hook inside.

I have no eyes. He can't control me, because I feel no pain, and I have no fear. The worst has already happened to me.

I am the fastest of the changed.

I am the strongest.

I squeeze his legs. Wood splinters under my fingers. I rip them out of their sockets, first the right, then the left. I throw them into the fire. Then I pry his hands out of my mask. It's easy after I crush his wrists. Rip his arms out with fat round *CLOK* sounds, burn them. I let the rest of his body fall to the floor.

I don't know if he's scared or angry. He's a doll, he was *made* a doll, by whatever power did this to all of us, and that power decided to strip everything away from him. Emotion. Voice. Empathy. And now he can't move, either, because I took that from him, too.

I stand over him. He killed Jeffrey. My best friend. My Jeffrey.

We all take from each other. We take and take and take.

"I don't understand why you did this," I say, "but I can't feel sorry for you."

He stares at me, unblinking. I bring my heel down on his head like a piston.

His head pops. The noise is something I've heard before, in a memory that hasn't yet returned. It's an explosion. His forehead spins in one direction, his jaw another. Teeth scatter like Tic Tacs.

His eyes roll away, the small red laserbeams fading. There is blood inside him, like in the rest of us, and my leg is coated in it.

I fall to my knees, catching a glimpse of my reflection in the floor.

I see my face. My mouth. Snarling. Lined with fangs. They are small knives, gleaming steel, flashing.

What did this to me?

The answer comes as a baseball bat to the back of my head.

.33......

I am underwater.

I am drowning.

When I went back to school, Principal Mitchell and Vice Principal Kaur were waiting to speak to me in the administration office. The video was very close to underage pornography, they said.

They wanted to know if I had put the video up. Panic so terrible washed over me I couldn't breathe, couldn't think. Finally I said, No, I didn't, I would never have done that.

Then they asked if I knew who might have.

I told them Jake and Shondra and Raph and their friends. Because, why not?

They said they'd already spoken to Jake and Shondra and

Raph and their friends, and none of them knew anything about it apart from that they had shared the video online. They were having their prom tickets revoked for bullying. No suspension, no detention. Just no prom.

No prom would definitely stick with them for the rest of their lives. No prom would definitely define their futures and haunt them for the rest of their days.

Then Principal Mitchell asked if I understood that I could get suspended for public indecency, for having sex at school.

I told them I hadn't had sex at school.

They asked if I had a risk-taking personality.

I told them it was very much the opposite.

The school counselor came in next. I had to answer a lot of questions about my home life and life at school and my relationship with Jeffrey. Principal Mitchell said they had reported this to my parents, just this morning. The world blurred into a horror of colors and sounds.

I was allowed to leave at lunch. I wandered into the cafeteria, sat down without getting food. I stared at the table. Eventually Jeffrey sat down beside me. All he had on his tray was some applesauce.

Raph Johnson walked by and whistled at us. *Hey, kitty cat and Jefferson. When's the next episode coming out? I'd like some more of that hot art room action!*

A few kids laughed. My body flickered between hot and

cold. I clutched the edge of the table until Raph was gone, then stood and hurried from the cafeteria, down the main hallway, out of the building. I hunched over the shrubs by the front walk, but I didn't have anything to throw up. Freezing January wrapped itself around me. Snow settled in my hair. My fingertips were already turning red. I considered walking home in the snow, and if I happened to fall dead in a ditch on the side of the road, it was probably for the best.

Footsteps crunched behind me. I looked up, expecting Jeffrey.

It was Ryan Lancaster. His perpetually bandaged hands were stuffed in the pockets of his torn-up parka. Underneath the parka was a tuxedo, like he was going somewhere fancy. His brown hair was combed neatly to the side.

What are you staring at? I spat at him, very aware of the snot and the tears dripping down my face. Did you watch the video, too? What did you think? Like it?

He didn't say anything.

What do you fucking *want*, Ryan? I'm never going to have a normal life, because this is going to be in my head. Forever. This is the kind of shit that never ends. I'm not going to wake up one day and all these memories are gone. I can't even change my name and move to another country to fix this kind of thing, because it will *always be with me*. I am *fucked, forever.* Fuck that. Fuck *you.*

I stood and shoved him out of the way. I could feel his eyes following me back to the front doors.

I sat through the rest of my classes in silence that day. It was over. Everything was over. There was no point. No point to school, or to trying to get my painting into that scholarship competition. No point in trying to understand anyone else.

The world wasn't created to make sense, and I was finished trying to find some in it.

That afternoon I went to the art room to get the painting I was working on. When I grabbed my brushes from my cubby, one caught on the corner of the sheet that still covered my ruined oil painting. Half a year of dust whuffed into the air.

I grabbed the sheet and ripped it off.

It hadn't changed. It never would. I'd show it to my mom and explain what had happened, and she and Dad would be understanding, but they wouldn't understand. And they definitely wouldn't understand the video. They'd look differently at me. Forever.

I rested my forehead on the edge of my cubby until I steadied my breathing. Grabbed my current painting and headed out of the art room.

I would leave.

I would go home.

I would try to explain it to my parents. At least *try*.

I would . . . I didn't know what I would do anymore.

Pop pop

It was a strange noise. Far away, but inside.

Pop pop

The hallway was deserted. Maybe it came from the other side of the school. I headed to my locker to grab my coat.

Pop pop

It was not the noise of something breaking. It was the sound of small explosions.

I heard screaming. Mrs. Remley's door blew open. Someone stumbled out. Jeffrey. Hair disheveled, face flushed. He scrabbled across the floor, and when he saw me, he screamed.

Run!

A large red flower bloomed in the middle of his blue sweater vest; at its center was a round dark hole, hypnotic, abyssal. A tide of déjà vu told me I had seen that hole before, I would see it again, I had lived my whole life seeing it, watching it appear over and over, blooming red and blue petals. Jeffrey fell to his knees. Then onto his face.

Ryan Lancaster stood behind him with a gun in his filleted fingers. The gun was an assault rifle. The gun was a pistol. The gun was a bazooka. The gun was a toy.

Ryan stepped over Jeffrey's body. He had discarded his parka; his tuxedo was too large, like a costume, and flecked with blood. I stood motionless, my canvas held up as if it might protect me. I knew then what was happening, but it didn't seem real. The tuxedo made it silly. Cliché. Like bets to get someone on a date, or interviews in bad cop dramas, or getting killed by the slasher after sex.

They'd asked him when he was bringing the gun to school. Today. He was bringing it today.

Ryan stopped two feet from me, his expression as calm as it had been outside, standing in the snow.

He pointed the gun at my face. Rifle, pistol, bazooka, toy. The hole was bottomless.

I'm sorry for everything they did, Cat, he said.

Everything who did? I asked, breathless, though I already knew the answer.

Everyone; the world.

And then he shot me.

A THOUSAND LITTLE CUTS

I was shot and killed on a January day in the hallways of my high school. The gunner was Ryan Lancaster, a boy I had known since first grade. I am pretty sure he also killed my best friend, Jeffrey. I don't know how many others he murdered. I don't know why he did it. I don't know why he apologized to me at the end.

Jake's bat connects with my head and knocks me over. I roll and stop, righting myself almost instantly.

"You did this!" Jake screams, lunging at me.

I duck.

"You got them all killed! You had to wake up that *thing*, and now everything's gone to shit!"

Everything has been shit. We just never knew.

A thick lacquer of blood covers half of Jake's face. His eyes burn. The walls are expanding outward rapidly now, taking the fire and the bleachers and everything else with them.

"Everyone's dead! Shondra, Raph—"

"Jeffrey?" I spit. "Didn't forget your own brother, did you? You didn't forget what you did to him?" Jake swings the bat again and I grab it, tear it from him. It isn't easy to do—he's strong— but it turns out I'm stronger. I hurl it across the floor.

I am anger. I am violence. It's only the two of us here now, no more weapons, no more distractions. "I remember what happened," I say. "Before all of this. I remember school, I remember my painting, I remember the video. I remember having my fucking face shot off. Do you remember, Jake? Do you remember what it felt like when everything was ripped away from you?"

He backs away, hands held up in defense. I crave his fear, yet I am not satisfied by it. It's not enough to fill this horrible void inside me.

The walls and ceiling are gone, and the fire is a small line in the distance. What light there is comes from the mirrored floor beneath us.

"Did you ever *have* anything ripped away from you?" I ask, striding to keep pace with him. "Or did you enjoy taking things from other people for the fun of it? Did you do it for the sport?"

He punches at me and I grab his hand and shatter it. Jake screams; he holds his stump to his chest and stumbles backward.

"Please," he says, "please, Cat . . . "

"Are you *begging*? Do you expect me to show you mercy? When have we ever been merciful to each other? Any of us?"

He stumbles over his own shoes and falls. I'm on top of him instantly, my hands at his throat. My claws shred and slice. He tries to push me off and can't. I feel as if I have waited for this moment for a hundred years. He is finally under my control.

I understand now where that particular brand of hatred comes from. It comes from a thousand little cuts over time. Sometimes people don't realize they're hurting you. But sometimes they do, and as they stick the knife in, they laugh and tell you it's just a joke.

Then one day you both die, and what was it all for?

I don't crush Jake's throat right away. I let my claws dig in while I press down with my palms, and I watch his face as he realizes there's nothing he can do. He knows he's going to die. He sees the end.

"Laserbeams wasn't the thing to fear, Jake," I whisper to him.

The light in those pretty green eyes starts to flicker.

Then something in his face reminds me of Jeffrey. The Jeffrey I used to know. Soft steel and honeypillar eyebrows. The boy who used to tell me stories about being little and playing catch in the backyard with his dad and his brother and their two big dogs, before his dad left and his mom started paying too little attention to both of them and too much attention to the friends she invited over for parties. Jeffrey before he was ruined. Or maybe not. I'm not convinced we aren't ruined by being born. All of us.

I release Jake and fall back, my hands shaking, my arms shaking, everything shaking because I wanted to kill him. I wanted to kill him not because I had to but because I wanted to, and I almost did it. Jake writhes on the floor, struggling to lift himself up.

"He's dead," I gasp through shallow breaths. "They're all dead. *We're* all dead."

Jake holds his throat and watches me.

I look down at my hands. Claw-knives and blood. I have become violence. "What was this all for? Why were we put here? Is this supposed to be hell? Are we being punished?"

"I don't think it's *us*," he says finally. "I think it's *you*."

.34......

It hurts, it hurts, it hurts
    I just don't want to hurt anymore

FLOWER VALLEY

I look up. A little girl with straight black hair and a featureless face is looking at me, though she has no eyes. She speaks, though she has no mouth.

"You're not being punished," she says. She pulls her knees up to her chest and wraps her arms around them, like we're having a friendly conversation on a green lawn somewhere. She wears a pretty blue dress and black saddle shoes. "You're being taught."

"Taught *what*?" I ask. "That we're horrible to each other? That we'll all die and be alone?" I motion to what's left of School around us. Everything is black except for the circle of mirrored floor we sit on. The word "alone" echoes into the darkness.

I can't breathe. "Why did I remember now? Why, after all this time?"

"Has it been all this time?" the girl asks. "Or has all this time been only now?"

I don't understand her, and then, slowly, I do.

I began when my memories did. I am here to remember.

The girl says, "Take off the mask, Cat."

"I can't," I cry. "It doesn't come off."

"Yes, it does," she says.

I want to take it off. But my hands are mangled claws and my arms won't move. All my speed and strength are gone. I've used them up in my hatred and my violence and have none left for this one simple thing.

"I need help," I say.

After a moment's pause, the girl stands, walks over. She takes my hands and pulls me to my feet. She's tiny, maybe five or six.

"There," she says. "You can do the rest."

When my hands find my face, I let them rest there, claws scraping against the fangs in my mouth, the empty holes where my eyes used to be. I want eyes, I want teeth and a tongue and lips. I want to breathe and speak.

I grab at the edges of my mask. It feels as if it's sealed tight because it isn't just a mask. It's my own flesh, hardened.

I pull.

There is pressure, and then the whole thing cracks away all at once, like a scab picked from a wound. Cool air rushes in beneath it. The mask falls to the floor, where I see my face—the face I remember—before the blood-spattered mask lands between our feet and shatters.

Like a rock thrown into a pond, it creates a circular ripple that travels out into the blackness. Where it flows, flowers sprout. Blue chrysanthemums. Out and out and out. The petals glow in the dark as if they are lit from below.

.35.......

A final bright flash.

It is simple.

It is good.

What would you have named me? I asked my mom one night.

She was busy pruning her favorite juniper in the room behind the shop. Up on her work table, even with its trunk twisted over and around itself, the tree stretched well above her head.

She had been complaining again about my name. Catherine. The name Dad's family wanted me to have, because it was a family name. Tradition.

Mom thought for a moment, then said, I don't know.

You don't know? How can you get angry about it if you didn't have an alternative?

Oh, I *had* alternatives, she said, but I don't know now which one of them I would have chosen. Nothing on my list makes me think of you as you are now.

I didn't think the question was that complicated, I said.

She never took her eyes off her work, but her half smile contained her good humor. I wanted you to have a name that fit. One that you were proud to have, one that made you feel like yourself. I'd have let you pick your own, but it would have taken a while for you to get to that point, and I couldn't leave you nameless for the first years of your life.

I sat up. Why did you paint *Catherine* on my wall, then? If you didn't like it?

She nipped off a shoot of juniper.

I didn't want you to think there was anything wrong with it. I wanted you to think it was beautiful. I might have once wanted to name you Lily, or Rhiannon, or Olivia, but none of those would be you, either, because you didn't choose them.

So the real question isn't what you would have named me, but what I would name myself?

That's exactly it.

I paused, watching her hands move.

I like Cat, I said.

THE BLINDING

"See?" the girl said. "That wasn't so hard."

I stare at the field of flowers. This is our sea, the one at the end of our river, the one we searched so long to find. The blue is infinite and complete; the flowers sway gently in a breeze from the darkness.

I touch my face. My skin is soft. My eyes are there. My lips are chapped, but I don't mind. I wear my black sweater, my jeans. A pair of soft socks.

"I don't understand," I say.

The girl tucks her hands behind her back and swishes her dress side to side. "You don't understand what?"

"What now? Is this . . . is this it?" I gesture around.

"I don't think so," she says. "Not unless you want this to be it."

I bend down and pick a chrysanthemum. Its petals spread a little wider for me, like they're drinking in sunlight.

"But why did this happen?" I ask.

"I don't know," the girl says.

"Why did Ryan do that?"

"There are probably a bunch of reasons. I'm not sure."

"What about my parents?"

"They loved you a lot. I am sure of that."

It isn't fair. None of this is fair.

"No, it isn't," she says, like she read my mind. "Fairness is something people made up to feel better about being alive."

I try so hard not to crush the chrysanthemum, but my hands are shaking. "Isn't there something I can do? Can't I go back? Start over, do better this time?" Like the stories, like the movies, like the books. There's always a second chance. There's always a do-over. It's a cliché, but don't clichés exist for a reason?

The girl shakes her head.

I feel lost, but there is no one left who can find me. There is only me.

When I can speak again, I say, "If I can't go back, where do I go?"

"Forward," the girl says. Her eyes are dark, her cheeks round and pink. I had scrubbed her face from my memory. It is painful and familiar. It's familiar because it's mine; I once wore that dress and those shoes.

Light spills over us. I turn. Behind me, a door has opened in the darkness. Through it is the pure white of the Blinding.

"That's all I have to do?" I say.

"That's it," she replies.

"Where does it go?"

"I don't know. I've never been there."

I look at it again. Maybe there's another nightmare waiting for me, but I know if I stay here, I will be in *this* nightmare forever.

I turn to the girl and hold out my hand. "Are you coming?"

She seems to deliberate for a moment, then shakes her head.

"What? Why?"

"This is my home," she says. "I will always live here."

"But you don't have to! The door is right there."

She shakes her head again, smiles, and points to her feet. They're gone. Her legs are trunks and her roots disappear into the flowers. Now she is older, thirteen, wearing a summer dress. Her hair is a crown of black ribbons, wild with prickly juniper foliage and twisting branches. She has been lovingly shaped. Blue blossoms grow deep in the tangle.

"But it's dark here," I say, scared for her. She's too young. This place is too awful.

"Not so dark," she says, raising her arms. They become branches too, twisting and sprouting. She is seventeen, young and beautiful even for all her faults. Ribbons fall, gleaming. She smiles down at the chrysanthemums that light her from below. "I have these now."

She becomes still and silent.

"But—"

She does not answer.

I look at the door.

There are some things I will never know. I will never know who vandalized the painting of my mother, or who decided to put that video online. I will never know why Jake treated me the way he did. I will never know why Ryan Lancaster apologized for the world before he shot me, or what made him decide to do what he did. I will never know what Jeffrey and I could have been. I will never know how my life might have unfolded had none of that ever happened.

I will never know why so much potential had to be lost to such senseless misery.

I wipe the tears from my face and hold my chrysanthemum to my cheek. The flowers part before me, creating a path to the door.

I look back only once.

There is a tree where a girl once stood.

ACKNOWLEDGMENTS

Thank you to my friends. You have always been there for me, even when I didn't deserve you. You have made me a better person, and, hopefully, I can make others better people in return.

Thank you to my agent, Louise Fury; her assistant, Kristin; and the whole team at the Bent Literary Agency. You didn't give up on this weird-ass book, and I very deeply appreciate it. So many of my weird ideas would not happen without you.

Thank you to Virginia Duncan, Sylvie Le Floc'h, and everyone at Greenwillow Books. I've said it three times before now and I'll say it always: you all are amazing, and you make all my work better. I am so grateful for all of you.

Thank you to my sensitivity readers, beta readers, and author friends. Darci Cole, Brett Werst, Marieke Nijkamp, Rebecca Coffindaffer, and especially Christina Bejjani, who is just an all-around champ; thank you for not hating me when I don't message you back for a month and a half.

Thank you to my parents and my siblings for keeping me alive when I was little (and for teaching me things and taking care of me and generally caring about my wellbeing, I guess). You're all my favorite people. Thank you to Chad for existing and being a wonderful human and listening to me talk about this story even when it was definitely too scary for you. I know this and I love you.

And, most of all, thank you to Gus and Carl, the best boys in the whole wide world.